Bronagh Hunt was born in Belfast and now lives in Dublin with her husband, Paul, and her three children, Josh, Imogen and Noah. Josh is a sport-mad, future Olympian; Imogen wants to be an artist and lives in her own fantastical world and Noah, the baby, is the king of the castle. Bronagh loves yoga, chocolate (in copious amounts), afternoon tea and reading books.

For my wonderful mum in heaven, Geraldine Bronagh Mary. xo

Bronagh Hunt

The Yoga School

Austin Macauley Publishers™
London • Cambridge • New York • Sharjah

A CIP catalogue record for this title is available from the British Library.

ISBN 9781528945356 (Paperback)
ISBN 9781528971324 (ePub e-book)

www.austinmacauley.com

First Published (2020)
Austin Macauley Publishers Ltd
25 Canada Square
Canary Wharf
London
E14 5LQ

Chapter One
Work

The Dublin bay commute must be one of the most beautiful commutes in the world. The green dart train skirts along the coastline from Greystones into town until the sea is obscured from view at Sandymount. I read after I can't gaze at the sea anymore, but before that I soak it in. I breathe deeply and lose myself in the beauty of it. In bad weather, there are big, stormy grey and white waves flowing and crashing. In good weather, the sea is calm, smooth and soothing. Starting my morning this way always calms my thoughts and sets me up for the day. This and my thirty-minute rise and shine yoga routine. Yoga warms up my body and mind for the day ahead. I set up my mat right beside my bed the night before so that I can fall out of bed half asleep and get straight into it. I do my morning practice with my eyes closed so that I can hold onto my sleepy dreamlike state for as long as possible. I only open my eyes when I'm finished, cross-legged with my hands in prayer. I thank myself for taking the time to do the practice and set an intention for day. Some days it's about self-care, other days it's about not punching someone!

My day is always busy. I am a marketing manager in a big American technology firm. I've been working here for three years. My mother tells everyone how well I'm doing. I have a good salary, a team and prospects. She's very proud. I am less proud of myself. I feel like I am wasting my years and talents selling technology, but I'm super sensible and have grown comfortable with the lifestyle that my salary provides. Therefore, I am not going anywhere soon, even though my heart and gut frequently sends me signals that I could be doing something much more fulfilling and life enhancing.

Work has always been important to me. I work hard at school, at relationships and professionally. I am just that sort – a worker, a doer. Drilled into me by an over bearing mother, no doubt. On one hand, it has served me well in that I did well in school and college and now have a decent job, but I work too hard. I know I do. I struggle to relax and enjoy just being in the moment. Yoga is the one exception to that rule. I discovered yoga in college and have been hooked ever since. It is my physical and mental workout and also my escape from the world.

Because I spend so much time at work I even met my boyfriend at there. His name is Alex. Alex is the sales director of the company. He is extremely confident to my timidness, classic handsome to my quirky looks, super ambitious to my non-competitive nature. Mum and Dad think he's amazing. So do my friends who are all jealous of his penthouse apartment and his BMW. I like him because he likes me and I love him because he brings me out of myself and pushes me to be better than I am. I know my bitchy friends can't fathom the reason he's with me but I don't care. He is, so they can sod off.

It's Monday and the day stretches out like many other Mondays with my team one to ones, weekly planning and the mind-numbing management meeting this afternoon. My intention this morning was to be more positive because I find Mondays particularly tough. I must be positive! Perhaps today will be much more exciting than all the other preceding Mondays. Let's see how long my positive attitude lasts!

As I hit the reception of the office I am met with, "Hey, Ellie, how was your weekend?" It's the receptionist. A mega party girl, she wants to hear about drunken exploits so I omit telling her about doing a yoga class and the two books I read and instead opt for, "Great thanks. Too many margaritas and too short as always. What about you?"

"Oh, mental as usual. I was in Coppers until all hours!" She fake pukes and makes a popeyed vomit face. We are pleasant to each other in a colleague sort of way but we are not friends. I think we'd both rather chew our arms off and beat ourselves with them rather than spend an evening alone together. Smiling, I excuse myself and head for my section which is on the second floor, back left by the window. It is a coveted a spot because it is near the coffee station and it has a view of the canal. There are frequently swans and ducks playing and gliding past. It's quite lovely. Many a more senior person has eyed my desk and section and made noises about moving the office around but so far I have thwarted all attempts to be moved. I'm late (as usual), so my team is already there. Narinda, PR manager, curvaceous, feisty and loyal as they come. Mark, Digital Manager, bitchest, most groomed man on the planet, and Molly, Communications Manager, pretty, sweet and beautifully blonde. They are a great team and I love working with them. I'm less of a boss and more like one of the group. I pull for them and them for me. It's just the way I like to do it.

"Hello, girls and boys, how are we all this wonderful morning?" Grunts all round. They sound like I feel. I will be extra nice to them today and try to spread my positive vibe intention.

Settling at my desk I appraise it happily. My desk is my little haven. Everything is perfectly pretty and orderly. I won the battle for a MacBook instead of a PC, so my laptop is white and beautiful. Yesterday I came in for a few hours to catch up and put my weekly fresh flowers on my desk. Cream and blush roses this week. I got them at the flower market yesterday morning. It's the best place to buy flowers although it does been a 6am start but looking at them now, it was worth it. These ones will last all week. I replaced the standard work chair and bought my own in, which people think is weird, but I have a bad back and the office chairs are rubbish. This chair is from my gran's house. It's an old-fashioned padded chair with a straight back. Originally, it was orange and green velvet, which was kind of gross and not my style so I had it professionally painted and reupholstered to a lovely, soft pink, grey and cream pinstripe with matt silver buttons. My desk area sticks out a mile in the sea of black chairs and laptops. People here think I am weird and a bit crazy, which I guess I am compared to them. I have always been slightly offbeat and quirky in my tastes. This suits my manner and my look. I have an abundance of brown unruly, curly hair that reaches down to my waist. My mother calls my mane, my one beauty. Cheers Mother! She is a special woman. Only she could wrap a compliment in a criticism. My very large emerald eyes and small pale oval face complete a look that is akin to a mythical pixie or fairy. I know that I'm not traditionally beautiful, but I get attention because I'm unusual, I guess.

"Ready for my 121, boss lady?" smirks Mark.

"Absolutely. Been dreaming about it since last week! Where shall we have it today? Barbados, Antigua, Mexico or meeting room three?"

Mark laughs, "I hear meeting room three is lovely this time of year and there is a spectacular view of the car park!"

And so the day begins. It's not a bad Monday, really. Just the management meeting to survive before I can make a break for freedom. As I sit in the boardroom, I have to pinch myself hard so that I don't fall asleep. This involves driving my nails into the fleshy skin between my thumb and fingers. I hate numbers and analysis and charts. I stare at the PowerPoint screen like everyone else, but I'm totally zoned out thinking about where I might go on my next holiday. I have three marketing update slides, but otherwise the meeting is utterly pointless and a total waste of time for me. My boyfriend Alex is there as well. As the sales director, he is really into the detail of all the numbers and is one of the main contributors to the meeting. He'll ask me later about his 'performance' and whether I agreed with him. I'll tell him that he was brilliant and totally right in his thought process, but really, I was in my own world and haven't the foggiest clue what is going on. The world in my head is a much more fun place to dwell than the reality in this boardroom.

I have a yoga class after work at my favourite studio, Acorns. It is only a ten-minute walk from home. I like to get changed at the office so that I can shed my work self, with enough time to transition into a good headspace before my class. Tonight is the energetic, Vinyasa class. Vinyasa is a term that describes many different styles of yoga. It essentially means, movement synchronised with breath and is a vigorous style based on a rapid flow through sun salutations. The teacher is a fiery, Spanish lady with a reputation for really pushing her students. I enjoy being pushed, since it is hard to push yourself in private practice. This is my energetic, sweaty class of the week. I like to do it on a Monday to kick-start my week. On Wednesday, I do Iyengar Yoga at a small studio in a lady's house. This class helps me with postural alignment as Iyengar has an emphasis on detail and precision in the performance of posture and breath control. Friday, I celebrate the weekend with a stretch and relax class, and I sometimes manage a restorative class on Sunday evening if I'm feeling a bit under the weather and need some rest. I love yoga. Among its many benefits, It helps calm my mind, which is no easy feat when my brain tends to go at a pace of a hundred miles per hour. This evenings class does not disappoint. I am sweaty, stretched, lightened and happy as a walk home. Super end to the day. Bring on Tuesday.

Chapter Two
Alex

"What shoes do you think I should wear with this outfit? The black or the brown ones?" Alex proffers the two pairs in front of my face. I have been ready to leave for thirty minutes but as usual he is still getting ready. Talk about role reversal!

I roll my eyes theatrically, "Does it really matter? Who is going to be look at your shoes anyway?"

He scoffs at me, "I always look at a guy's shoes. They say everything about a person. For example, those uggs that you're wearing have seen better days and don't do anything for your outfit or figure which makes me think that you don't give a crap."

"About what I wear to your mum's house for a casual visit? Yeah, I don't give a crap, neither will your mum."

Why are we arguing about something so petty? Did I start this or did he? It doesn't matter, I will pacify the mood. As always.

"You look great. I think the brown is best as it complements the green jumper."

Alex frowns and looks at the shoes, "Really? Mmmh, I think I'll go with the black." He is unbelievable. So vain. I've never met a man like him. I like what I like in terms of clothes. I don't follow fashion or trends. Some of my clothes date back a decade. Alex on the other hand is a clothes horse. I don't think he wears a shirt more than twice and his wardrobe is immaculate. Mine on the other hand is more like The Lion, the Witch and the Wardrobe!

When we finally leave the house, he insists on driving his car as it's faster and posher than mine. His brother might be at his mum's and he wants to show him the sound system or something. As we wizz through South Dublin and along the M-50 to Castleknock, where he is from, I stare out the window thinking about the feast that awaits us. His mum, Janice is lovely. Whenever anyone visits, she bakes and her baking is to die for. I especially love her Carrot Cake and Victoria Sponge, so my fingers are crossed for one of these. His Mum and Dad divorced when he was about ten. His Dad remarried a lady from Chile and moved there, so Alex doesn't see him at all. He gets the occasional random text, but otherwise there is no relationship there. His mum on the other hand is an amazing lady and a force to be reckoned with. She is a Home Economics teacher at the local secondary school and has a small catering business on the side, mainly doing Christenings and parties. She is a wonderful cook and host. I love visiting her house. When we pull up on the drive she rushes to the door and is ready with big, warm hugs and a smile that would put the world to rights.

"So lovely to see you both. You both look great, if a little on the slim side. I have been baking so let's see if we can put some meat on those bones."

Alex scowls, "I'm on a very tightly controlled nutrition plan. I'm half a stone off my target weight, so I can't have any carbs today and definitely no sugar." Janice looks at Alex, wounded for a nanosecond and then plasters the smile on again. "Well, all the more for me and Ellie then."

Janice has outdone herself. A Victoria sponge, carrot cake, and a lemon drizzle, which is Alex's favourite. I watch him drooling over it and inwardly laugh, knowing that he now regrets his little monologue about the diet. Hilarious! I intend to have everything and bring some home in a box that I have brought with me, knowing from experience that there would be leftovers.

"How is the yoga going, Ellie? Not left work yet to pursue it fully?" She is half joking, half not. I have talked to her before about my dream of being a yoga teacher. I qualified a number of years ago and have been doing some light teaching since, but haven't really committed to it.

"I'd love to Janice. It's just the insecurity of it. You don't become a yoga teacher for the money as it pays so little and unfortunately I can't afford it."

She pats my hand and smiles, "I know it's hard hon, but money isn't everything. Happiness is the most important thing. You'll be long enough dead. You should do something that you love rather than something you feel you should do."

Janice is so loving and nurturing. She is quite unlike my own mother who I love of course but is a weapon! While we have been chatting, Alex has broken his no sugar and carb ban and is tucking happily into a huge wedge of lemon drizzle. We both laugh and smile at him. He looks up and beams, shrugging his shoulders. I catch a hint of the carefree, well fed, happy boy he must have been and wonder when he changed and became so serious. His dark mood broken, he laughs and jokes with his mum asking her about her job, her health and the house. In these moments, I like to stay quiet and just watch and listen. Study him. He really is a good guy, but he sometimes masks it with bravado, moodiness, designer labels and attitude. Perhaps he acts like that because he thinks he needs to. I love him most, like this in his Mum's kitchen eating cake. All the trappings of success mean nothing to me. I wish he was like this more often.

For the rest of the day, he is a dream and we have the loveliest time that I ever remember us having. Fish and chips on the freezing cold beach. Throwing stones in the sea. He can throw the stones further, but I persist, and he laughs loudly loving how focussed I am in trying to beat him. We have ice cream even though it's freezing just because we want to. We end up having to run back to the car because of a sudden downpour. We are drenched through, but it doesn't matter. We sing at the top of our voices to eighties pop all the way home. After a long hot shower together to rid ourselves of the damp rain we have unusually gentle sex. Alex is normally more domineering; he likes it fast and rough. I don't mind, I love him and he's seriously hot so going along with how he likes it is fine with me. I haven't had that many boyfriends, so I don't really have a preference. It's more about being close and connected for me, but I have to admit, this gentle, caring side of him is lovely. I really don't ever recall feeling so happy and in love with him.

Chapter Three
Uncovered

I was due to go home to Mum and Dad's this weekend. I haven't been back in ages. Mum has been badgering me for weeks to visit so I relented. Alex couldn't come with me as he has a big presentation on Monday and must prepare for it. I had the car packed so I could head off straight from work but at lunch Mum called to tell me not to come because she got a last-minute invitation to some church training course. I feel like I've been given a monopoly get out of jail free card. So instead of a long drive to see the parents I can surprise Alex and enjoy a weekend with no plans at home. I've been so busy lately that this prospect sounds like bliss.

As I nearly fall in the doors of the apartment building with my grocery shopping, laptop bag and work files, I mouth a hasty hello to the concierge who is called Bill. He is a really nice guy, if not a tad lazy. I think he spends much of his time watching Netflix and reading the paper but fair play to him if he's happy. He looks at me strangely, in a different way from usual cheery manner. He looks a bit perplexed actually. He nods hello and quickly looks down at the paper in front of him. Mmmh, that's a bit odd. Maybe he's had a bad day. He's usually so friendly. You'd think he'd offer to help with all my stuff!

I stumble on through reception and lean against the wall beside the lift barely able to press the button with my little finger. When it comes, I'm the only person in it thankfully, so I unceremoniously dump all my stuff on the floor with a loud crash and press for number eight. I have a few moments rest. I cannot wait to open a bottle of wine. I hope Alex has one in the fridge. By the time we drink that one, the one I've just bought will be nicely chilled. In my grocery bags are some yummy treats from Marks and Sparks, but maybe I won't cook, maybe we'll just order something in. Some nice Thai. Pad Thai would be yummy. I'll cook the stuff I bought tomorrow instead. I'll see what Alex wants to do.

The lift pings open, let's go and move all this nonsense baggage again. I lift my laptop bag and work files but move the rest by pushing, slash kicking the bags with my feet. Not terribly ladylike, but no one's around so who cares. Keys are in the very bottom of my bag of course! My bag is always a nightmare. Everyone laughs at me. I have everything in this bag but I can never find anything! Such a jumbly, rumbly mess. I really need to sort it out one of these days. Hurray! Found the damn keys. Here we go. I continue to kick the bags in the door. I'll go back and close the front door, when I've dumped everything on the kitchen floor.

As I go into the kitchen, a sight awaits me that I will never forget. Alex is totally naked from the waist down in the throes of shagging his assistant who is lying naked on the kitchen island unit. Beside him is another girl from the office. She is stripped to her bra and pants, and is gyrating against him, kissing him and pulling on his nipples while he shags bint number one. There are clothes everywhere. Champagne glasses and the Moet I was saving for a special occasion are empty and dis-guarded on the living room rug. There is a smell of cigarettes and really loud music. I fixate bizarrely on the cigarettes. I'm especially annoyed by them for some reason. I hate smoking. How could he let them smoke in our home? Backup, Ellie, he's having a fucking orgy in your kitchen. It's like something from a nightmare that I could never have imagined. They don't see me at first so they continue as they are but then I deliberately throw all my crap on the floor loudly. They stop and look around. The girls, to their shame don't look shocked, embarrassed or remotely bothered. They are actually smirking. What little bitches. Fucking karma better bite their tiny little asses one day.

Alex is aghast, horrified and frantic.

"What are you doing here?" he shouts.

"What do you mean, what am I doing here? I live here. This is my home. What the fuck are YOU doing?" I spit the words out. I am the angriest I have ever been. In this moment I understand how normal and nice people could kill. There is a knife block on the side with very sharp knives. Alex insists on sharpening them once a month. Wouldn't it be funny now to be killed with one of his own obsessively, sharp knives?

He pushes the girls away from him and stares darkly at me, "I didn't think you were coming back today, I thought you were going to your parents," he says.

"Oh, and that makes it all right, does it? I'm due to be away and you think it's okay to have a fucking orgy in our apartment," I scream, like a banshee woman. I scream in his dark gorgeous face because he has wounded me to my core and I am like a possessed woman. He looks annoyed. Fucking arsehole. He speaks very quietly, "You're overacting, Eleanor."

He has never ever called me by my full name. Nobody does. Not even my stuffy mother. His use of it now totally incenses me, "I'm overacting! You have some nerve you dirty, cheating, lying bastard. What the fuck! Get these little slags out of here right now. Right now. Do you hear me?"

I never swear. I hate swearing, but in this moment this is the only vocabulary that can come close to matching my emotions. I can't be in the kitchen any longer so I go out to the balcony. On my way, I grab a bottle of wine from the Marks bag. It's a screw top thankfully, so I unscrew it and start chugging it down like lemonade on a hot day. It's revolting and I gag repeatedly. I can't believe this is happening to me. I'm a good person. We were fine. How could he even have it in him to do this to me? Is that really the kind of sex he likes? Is this the first time? Couldn't be! It all looked far too familiar. He looked way, way, way too comfortable in the scenario. How could I be so stupid? So blind. What the hell am I going to do?

I few minutes later, Alex emerges fully dressed in a hoodie and sweatpants. He looks so normal now. Did it really happen, or did I black out and have a nightmare? Looking past him, I see the tell-tale remains of the orgy and my stomach lurches. Of course it happened. I'm not sure if it's shock or the gross wine, but I vomit violently for a few minutes. Alex holds back my hair. When I'm done, I explode into a mess of hysterical sobbing and he pulls me into his lap and holds me like a child, stroking my hair. I let him because I love him and I don't want this to be happening, and because I want him to go back to being the boy eating cake in his mum's kitchen, not the man who is breaking my heart. After what seems like hours, I stop crying and we are silent. Still enveloped around each other on the floor of the balcony. I realise that I'm freezing and start to shiver. He feels it and lifts me up in his arms and carries me inside. He sets me gently on the sofa and wraps my favourite grey throw around me. I bought it in a market in Morocco, when he took me there for my birthday as a surprise. I've always wanted to go. It was an extremely thoughtful gift. It was on that trip that he asked me to move in with him. For the first time since my shouting outburst, I look at him. He can't meet my eye. Won't look at me.

"Do you have nothing to say?" My voice is small, faraway. I don't recognise myself. Funny how that happens in a few short moments. You can change. Be forever changed. An hour ago, I was happy.

"Oh, Ellie." He still doesn't look at me. "I know it's bad. Really bad. I'm sorry you saw what you did, I really am, but it's just sex. It doesn't mean anything. Men and women think differently about it. They're just slags that like sex. They don't mean anything. They aren't you. I know it's a shock, but we can move on from this. I know we can."

I am so confused by what he's saying. He's sorry but he's justified. It's like if I hadn't seen it, it would have been fine. And even though I hate those girls, I am offended and sickened that he referred to them as slags.

"What planet are you on? It's so not okay. I can't forget what I saw. It is NOT okay. You are not the person I thought you were. We can't come back from this. I can never trust you again." These words just fall out of my mouth. I know them to be true and I sound strong and resolute, but my heart is broken and yearning for him to beg and plead for my forgiveness. To say he can't live without me. To say it was a crazy error in judgement and that he will spend the rest of his life making it up to me.

But he doesn't say any of these things. Instead he stands up, folds his hands over his chest and says, "Well then, you better get your things and go."

My eyes must be like saucers. "I should go? You did this to me. To us. You should go." He looks really stern and mean. Like he does in tough meetings at work.

"This is my apartment, Ellie. I asked you to move in, but it is mine. I would prefer that you stayed and that we worked this out, but if you can't get past this then you should go." Where is that fucking knife block. I should have finished him off when I had the chance. He is no longer Alex to me. He will forever be – The Bastard.

Chapter Four
Sacked

I'm all over the place. One minute I'm thinking, fucking bastard I'm never going to speak to him again, darkly wishing and fantasising about his painful death, and then the next minute I'm sobbing my heart out, remembering all the nice things that he did. I guess it's love, but it's so destructive. I always go for people that are wrong for me. Always go for people who really don't give a shit about me, who always choose another person over me in the end. I always return to this same horrid cycle. It's like I want to hurt myself. Maybe I want to be hurt. Maybe I am incapable of happiness.

I am absolutely dreading going back to work imagining seeing him and the two girls. I just feel so degraded and bruised, but I have to man up and go. It's my job, I have a career and bills to pay. So, after two pretend sick days spent crying under a duvet in a cheap hotel, I steel myself and make sure I look as good as humanly possible for me. I am wearing my best work outfit, a figure hugging Karen Millen dress with gleaming black, patent stilettos. Perfect hair and flawless makeup. All this gives me a confident look that belies the truth. This will be the best performance of my life so far. I generally wear my heart of my sleeve. My every thought and emotion are plastered for all to see on my face. I don't go in for games or acting. I am who I am. However, today I need to be like steel. I need to act today. I can fall apart later but I must make it through this day. He will not ruin all aspects of my life.

Although my world was completely upside down, everything in the office seemed normal. Not sure what I expected, but the status quo is weird. When I get to my desk, someone has already been there as there was a post-it note saying, "JC wants to see you ASAP." JC is the Managing Director. He doesn't speak to me very often, so I'm surprised by the summons. Perhaps he wants me to organise the sponsorship of his yacht club or wife's tennis team. That's embarrassingly happened before. He frequently pillages my marketing budget, using his position to bankroll his loaded friends' hobbies. It annoys me, but hey, I am but a minion in this place. I must respond to the summons quickly, since he doesn't like to be kept waiting. So, I unenthusiastically grab my notebook and pen, and head for his ridiculously huge office. It's in the corner and has an amazing view of the docks. He even has his own wraparound balcony. I notice it has sun loungers on it. A bit much for work I think and also it's Ireland mate, you'll be lucky to sit on them once a year! His bitchy little secretary isn't in yet, so I just knock on the door. That's a small mercy, since she's like a little Hitler with her power over his diary and whereabouts. He is on the phone, but he ushers me to take a seat. As I wait, I unfortunately see the bastard arriving through the glass office walls. He is laughing with two of his boy chums and sipping his usual morning coffee. Decaf latte with three shots of coffee. I hate that I know that. I hate that he's laughing with not a care in the world. What a bastard! I am snapped from my dagger staring because JC finishing his phone call.

"Ellie, thanks for coming to see me." I brace myself for the embarrassing sponsorship ask or an inane conversation about some idea his daughter had for a social media campaign or something equally frustrating but what follows never entered my head.

"I'm afraid we are going to have to let you go. The board has been reviewing the structure and it is felt that there is no further need for a Head of Marketing. This will be treated as a redundancy; therefore you are entitled to a month's pay for every year you have worked plus your three months' notice. Given the circumstances I do not expect you to work that notice and after this conversation you will be escorted to your desk, where you can pack your things before leaving the premises. I'm sorry it isn't better news."

Whoa! I felt like I'd been hit by a bus. Second time in a matter of days! This can't be happening. I'm so shocked that I don't say anything. I just sit there with a mouth wide open to catch flies. How has this never been even hinted at? The rumour mill is rife here. There would have been a whisper of a review somewhere, surely. We've been hiring recently. Business is booming. We just acquired two new companies last quarter. My role is important, and my team is small. This makes no sense. I think all this, but don't vocalise it as I am so stunned. JC doesn't look me in the eye during his news and still doesn't. He looks quite unnerved, which is unlike him. He's normally the biggest personality in the room. Something feels off about this. You don't just get sacked. I've managed staff members through redundancy situations before and there is consultation and reviews, and everything is in writing and managed through HR. I note that there is no one else in the room. Having recovered from my initial shocked, stunned silence, I gather myself and fire questions at him.

"How could my role possibly be deemed not necessary? Surely there should be a proper process to this? Why was I not made aware that this was a possibility? My marketing budget has just been increased and in my last performance review I was deemed outstanding. I have no idea where this has come from and I would like some more clarity please." He was ill prepared for my tirade and just looks down at his desk. His response – that there was no more information. If I wished to discuss it further I could go to speak with Sara in HR, and she could outline the package in more detail. Luckily for him, his mobile rings and he excuses himself and ushers me out of the office. Standing outside his office, the room feels as though it is spinning. How could this happen?

I can't just have lost my job. A job that I'm good at. How could this happen?

As I glance across the office in my bewildered state, my eyes landed on Alex who was sitting in his office on his sofa, feet up on the coffee table, watching me. He grins smugly at me with a nasty glint in his eye. In that look I realise what's going on. I have just been sacked because he told his friend to do so. He and JC are as thick as thieves. I march across the office and bulldoze into his office, slamming the door behind me so hard that it shook nearly to breaking.

"I've just been fired."

He is as casual as you like, "I know."

I confront him, "Does this have something to do with you?"

The nasty smile appears again, "Of course. It has everything to do with me. You can't just leave me and get away with it. Us working together is intolerable now."

"Alex, you can't do this. It's not right."

"Watch me, Ellie. Watch me. I think you better go."

"I think I better go too, before I fucking kill you!" Slamming the door for effect this time, I stalk to my desk. On the way, I grab a random empty box from beside the photocopier. I sweep my possessions off my desk in one swift movement making a huge racket. I empty my desk drawers, put on my coat and lift my chair. I'm fucking taking my fucking chair. With the box, my bag and the chair I struggle to the lift. *Everyone* is looking at me, whispering. Perhaps the story will be that I totally went bat crazy in the office and stole a chair. I don't give a crap, I just want to get the hell out of here. No one offers to help me. Even my team, for whom I've bent over backwards for, baked for, bought thoughtful gifts for years for, are huddled together looking at me like I'm a toxic alien. Clearly the news of my exit has spread through the office like a virus as all bad gossip does. In the lift, I meet my dizzy, receptionist pal. Not the company I need right now. She laughs, "Why are you carrying your chair? Is it bring your chair to work day?"

She is doubled over in kinks of laughter at her own joke. It wasn't that funny.

"No. I've been sacked." She stops in her tracks, "What! Why?"

"They said it was to do with the board but I reckon it's more to do with my tosser of an ex-boyfriend shagging half the office and not liking my reaction to it."

She's quiet and looks at me with empathy, "I'm really sorry Ellie. I didn't know how to say this to you or if I should as we're not really friends, but he's worked his way around most of the office while he was with you. He's known for liking really filthy sex. No one goes with him more than once as he's so rough. He's a vile asshole and you're better off without him. I'm sorry I didn't tell you."

The lift doors open. She looks like she's about to cry. I decide to be the bigger person, "Don't worry about it. It wouldn't have made much difference had I known sooner or not. It doesn't matter anymore."

Once through the revolving doors and outside. I look back at the office that I've given so much of my life and myself to. My overwhelming feeling is anger at myself. How could I have been so stupid as to give so much of myself to Alex and the company and wasted so much time and energy? I have no job, no home and no place to go. What do I do now?

As if my fairy godmother heard this pathetic plea, from across the street I hear my name being called. I turn to see where it's coming from and it's my cousin, Angus, waving frantically and shouting. Bless him. He is the most brilliant but also the most uncool person I know. He dresses like an eccentric professor and has huge horn-rimmed glasses. Today he's sporting a three-piece tweed suit with maroon coloured shoes. He is a lawyer, an utter genius and a pet. When he crosses over to me, I am enveloped in a huge Angus bear hug. I can smell the humbug sweets that he keeps in all the pockets about his person.

"Hello, gorgeous girl. I haven't seen you in forever. I'm on my way to court and late as usual. Walk with me.

Although you seem a bit encumbered, is that a chair from Granny's house? How odd!"

I quickly give Angus a potted version of what has just happened. He is appalled. "Bastards. Bastards. Bastards, the lot of them. That is totally out of order and illegal might I add. They can't just sack you like that. No way. We're not taking this lying down. I'm going in to speak to them."

"Oh, Angus, you're a pet but don't, please don't."

He studies me and for a second I think he is going to bolt into the building despite my entreaty, but then thinks better of it and says, "Okay. We'll talk about it properly later and work out a plan of action. In the meantime, here's my key."

He hands me his house keys from his jacket pocket.

"Go to my house. Get yourself settled and have a gin or three and I'll see you tonight after work. It might be late but stay up and I'll grab a takeaway on my way home. Until then relax, chill out, speak to no one about it and we'll sort it out. They cannot treat you like this." With this, he looks at his watch and runs off. Literally! He is mega late for court now.

Chapter Five
Angus

"Okay, before we eat, have a look at these." He hands me two letters. "While I was in court, I got my assistant to write two letters. One for Alex and one for your firm. See what you think."

I read the firm one first. It is rousing to say the least. It covers Alex's exploits with half the office, his admission that my sacking was at his request as a revenge for my dumping him. The nature of the sacking, the handling of it, my excellent previous performance. It is a good letter albeit a bit embarrassing to see my mess of a life laid out in a legal letter. I thought the second letter to Alex was a bit much. "Angus, you can't possibly expect him to pay me money for loss of the apartment."

"Why not? You contributed to the mortgage for the entire time that you lived there and all the bills. I know this because we had an argument about it last Christmas as I thought you were being a mug. Which, it turns out, you were. He can't just evict you without cause. The least he can do is give you the deposit and a few months' rent so that you can find somewhere to live. He can't get away with this. To be honest, he might not even keep his job after his work antics."

I sincerely doubt that. "He's golden balls in there. He's untouchable."

"Ah, but I didn't give the letter to his Managing Director mate. I gave it to the chairman of the board. They will be required to investigate the situation thoroughly. He'll be in very hot water, golden balls or not."

“Ahhhh! What do you mean you *gave* it? I thought I was checking them now?” Angus looks slightly sheepish.

“Yes, well, I may have neglected to tell you that I delivered them personally tonight after court.”

“But what if I don’t want you to send them?” I am panicked thinking about all the possible ramifications.

“My dear cousin, sometimes other people know what’s better for you. Those that love you. I knew that by the time I came home you would have simmered and lost some of the fighting spirit and that there was no way you would have let me send these letters as they are. Am I right?”

I nod briefly. He continues, “You have been treated appallingly by Alex and your firm and you should be compensated accordingly. As your lawyer and as your dear favourite cousin I took matters in my own hands and I think you will thank me for it.”

“Do you think I’ll get my job back?” Angus laughs, snorts actually. It’s unbecoming.

“What? No. No way. You don’t want to work there. You can get another job. The point of the letters is to get you enough financial compensation so that you can take your time deciding what to do next.”

I breathe out. This isn’t what I was thinking at all. All the scenarios in my head involved going back to work. Going back to how things were before. As if reading my mind Angus says, “Ellie, there is no going back now. I’m sorry I’ve been in lawyer mode. I can’t imagine how you felt when you saw what you did in your flat or how you felt today in work. It’s truly awful. But you will recover from this. You will feel better. You will get a better job and meet a nicer boyfriend.” At this point I roll my eyes.

“Yes, that’s right, I never liked him. And for good reason it seems. No one liked him but he wasn’t a surprise, you always pick naff guys. Your choice in men is diabolical.”

I feign outrage.

“Every guy you’ve ever liked has been an asshole, and the guys you dated who were actually nice, you were mean to and ended things with them. You always liked the challenge of turning someone mean and not that bothered about you into an adoring angel, but it never works, and you get hurt. Every time. Time and time again. Always a cycle. In fact, you should go see someone about it."

"Thanks, Angus. I really needed that pep talk. I don't think my cycle or tastes are an issue anymore. I think I'll just stay single for a while. A long while. Let's change the subject, how's your love life?"

"It's good. Gemma's great."

Perhaps it's because he's just had a go at me or maybe I'm just a cow but I say, "You know she's just with you for your money?"

"Nice. Are you trying to get your own back?"

"No, I just worry about you."

"Well don't be. Sure, Gemma was initially interested in me for the money. Most of the girls I date are. But then she got to know me and realised that I was a nice guy and that I was quite funny in a geeky sort of way. I also try hard at my relationships, in every department because I have to."

Oh gross. "If you're talking about sex, please don't because I might vomit."

I laugh, so does Angus. "I'm a realist. I'm not a good-looking guy. I'm not cool or charming but I'm successful and nice and funny. I don't stay with the gold diggers anyway. It's okay to be attracted to power and wealth and someone doing well in life. That's part of who I am but not all of me. Gemma appreciates it all. Also, she's gorgeous if you hadn't noticed."

I laugh. "I had noticed. She's like Barbie on speed. But is she a nice person as well?"

He nods, "She is. She's really into kids, which I appreciate. Someday, I'd like to have a family so being with someone who loves children is important to me. She's thoughtful too. She remembers things like my favourite food, the author I read on holidays, the way I take my tea, my mum's birthday and a million other little things. That care and attentiveness is lovely. Plus, did I mention how gorgeous she is?!"

I consider this and we are quiet for a few beats as we sip our drinks. "What about the soul connection and one true love?"

Angus rolls his eyes, "This is why you have so many problems with men. You're looking for something that doesn't exist. You look for a level of depth that most people are incapable of. It's not realistic Ellie. People meet, they have a reasonably good time, enjoy each other's company and tolerate their annoying traits. They realise they can live together without killing each other. They get married and have kids. Then they rumble along until they die."

"That is so unromantic and it's not what I want."

"Well, if you insist on waiting for your elusive soul connect, you might end up as a very lonely old woman."

"Let's agree to disagree. Shall we have another drink?" He smiles at me, an amused smile.

Chapter Six
The Golden Oldies

I just lay in bed in a depressive black hole all Saturday. Angus was at a wedding of one of Gemma's beautician friends and was sending me photos all day of him and gorgeous girls. He was channelling the Hoff, which he thought was hilarious but in my current mood I found it intensely annoying especially as every time my phone beeped I stupidly hoped it was The Bastard pleading for forgiveness or work offering my job back which of course it wasn't. I ate my weight in crap food, raiding every possible cupboard in the house including Angus's unwanted presents' drawer where I happily found nothing that I'd given him but some marzipan, short bread biscuits and Italian biscotti past its sell by date which I scoffed. I watched all the Bridget Jones films, Love Actually, My Best Friend's Wedding and some Little House on the Prairie which was on Channel 4. I cried, sobbed, hiccupped and snorted my way through despair, anger, helplessness and loathing.

By Sunday morning, I felt like I'd run an emotional and physical marathon. I looked and felt a mess, but I have a longstanding Sunday morning commitment that I have never broken so I pull my sorry ass out of bed and shower. I turn the heat up as high as I can take it and stay in there for probably thirty minutes letting the water caress away the tears and tension of the previous few days. I use every expensive shampoo, lotion, cleanser that I can find. Gemma has left a lot of crap here for when she stays over, so there is plenty to play with. As I only have a limited selection of my clothes, I need to borrow an outfit of Gemma's. Angus said that she didn't mind and that I could take whatever I wanted. She even texted herself to affirm this, which was sweet of her. However, Gemma is a Barbie wannabe and I am the polar opposite, so as I look through her clothes I am becoming more and more panicked. It is a sea of pink and pastels, strappy tops and bodycon dresses. Finally I find something barely acceptable rolled up in the back of the wardrobe which is why I find myself in hot pink leggings and an oversized jumper which has, 'If you can't be a unicorn be a princess' emblazoned on the front. There is an image of a unicorn and a princess just in case you are a total twat and can't read!

My longstanding commitment is an elderly yoga class. I am a yoga teacher at Golden Oldies Nursing Home and this is my Sunday session. I take two classes, one for the active residents and one for the chair bound peeps. An odd way to spend a Sunday some might think but I have been coming here for years. My Granny was a resident for six years before she passed away a few years ago. Since her death I've continued to visit as a yoga teacher. It keeps me connected to her as I see her old friends every week and I know she would approve, as she was a big fan of my yoga pursuits. Much more than my 'real' career actually. She was the one who paid for my yoga teacher-training course and encouraged me to start teaching.

"Hey, Ellie, do you know that you look like a big pink twat?"

"Ah thanks, Arthur, ever the charmer. Good to know that you can still see." He chuckles away to himself. He is a very sweet old man who made my Granny laugh a lot. He is in my second class so will no doubt potter off now around all the other people in the class telling them that I'm dressed like a cupcake and have clearly lost my mind. Ah well! My first class is for the residents who are chair bound. The carers always have everyone ready for me arriving. Bernie and Phil are working today. They greet me warmly while regarding my outfit in an amused fashion.

"Are you a unicorn or a princess?" Bernie says with a cheeky smile.

I laugh, "I feel more like the creature from the black lagoon today, but hey, fake it till you make it, I always say. Unicorn it is!" It feels good to laugh and to be around people who know me and like me. Looking out at my class, I take a deep breath. Fifteen expectant faces stare back at me, therefore I will have to muster energy and joy for them, from somewhere as this is their yoga session and it's not fair to bring my awful week to bear on their special time. I start by asking if anyone has any new niggles or illnesses that I need to know about. Hilda says that her elbow is sore as she banged it on the bed rail. I gently thank her for telling me and suggest that she put a blanket under her arm to cushion it. Bernie sees to this for her. I start with some gentle stretching. When they are warmed up, I lead them through specially modified flow sequences just for the upper body. I push them quite hard and walk around modifying their positions as we progress. At the end, I lead them through a guided relaxation meditation, aimed at relaxing them thoroughly. As I guide them through the meditation, I also work my way from person to person giving them a quick head massage with some lavender oil. I love the scent of lavender. It was my Granny's favourite and now, mine. By the end of the class, at least five of the oldies are always asleep. Today is no exception.

My second class is held in the recreation room. The carers move back all the tables and chairs so that we have plenty of floor space for our mats. Some of the class are really into it and have bought their own yoga mats. I love seeing the individuality in their choice of mat. The ones that don't have their own mat use the green mats that I organised for the home through a community grant. I successfully applied for the grant from the local council and we were awarded enough to buy mats, blocks, belts and bolsters. I store everything in a cupboard at the back of the recreation room. I love this time on a Sunday when I can quietly setup my class in silence. The room is lovely with large sunny windows and warm yellow walls. I arrange the mats and accessories, setup my aromatherapy diffuser and candles and sort the music on my iPhone. Then, I sit in seated position on my mat channelling inwards as I wait for the class to arrive. When they show up, I am in for a treat. Arthur has indeed done the rounds and they have decided to have some fun at my expense as every single one of them is wearing pink even Arthur who has clearly borrowed a pink t-shirt from one of the ladies, which is too tight for him. The effect makes me belly laugh, loud and long. These lovely oldies have lifted my spirits. Karma at its finest. What funny, lovely souls. I thank them for getting the memo about the new class uniform and then we begin.

The class is more advanced and challenging than the chair yoga class. Some of the oldies are in great shape. They put me to shame. Connie, a five-foot two Glaswegian lady with chronic diabetes is the best. She always goes at the front and is so inspired by yoga that she practices every day in her room. I devised some sessions for her specially. Today I admire her warrior pose form and think, she really is a warrior. I love Sunday's. I love being with these wonderful people and I love sharing my passion. I'm not the most amazing teacher in the world as I have a lot to learn, but what I lack in experience I make up for in preparation, attention to detail and passion.

To my slight annoyance Angus has been a busybody and phoned ahead to Rose, my Granny's' old best friend. After yoga class she asks me to join her in her room for a cuppa. She says that Angus is worried about me. I can't ever refuse Rose anything, so after class I find myself sitting in a comfy easy chair with sweet milky tea and a chunky piece of carrot cake which is my favourite. I'm touched that she remembered. Her lovely daughter will have been instructed to add this to her weekly shopping list from M&S. Rose and Granny loved M&S. It's rubbed off on me too. Can't beat the good old Marks and Sparks. Reminds me momentarily of the uneaten Marks shop, which fell all over the kitchen floor last week. I shrug the thought away quickly.

The residents' rooms are lovely. They are like little studio apartments with floor to ceiling windows at one end which overlook the gardens. They can furnish them as they please. Rose was a dressmaker back in the day; therefore, she has a real flair for putting things together. Her room is gorgeous, it's like a spread from the Laura Ashley catalogue. I love seeing Rose as it reminds me of visiting my Granny. Granny's room was filled with family photos, and flowers. It always smelt heavily of flowers. Rose looks at me steadily over her teacup.

"I hear that you've had a bad week darling girl." I sigh and close my eyes. I had forgotten briefly about my shit storm of a life this morning, but now I am dragged back to reality.

"I really wish Angus would keep his neb out of my business."

Rose looks stern. "If he did that you would have nowhere to stay and you wouldn't have a jolly big settlement from work. So be more thankful to your cousin. He has only your best interests at heart. Your Granny would have been furious."

"Yes, I know. She wouldn't have liked him."

"I don't mean *him*, although she would have hated him. I mean she would be furious at you dear."

I did not expect this. I was all prepped for tea and sympathy not a lecture. I know I look shocked and offended but Rose continues undeterred, "You are easily the smartest, most creative, kind, gifted person I know, yet you seem intent on a life mission to sabotage yourself. Your career is pointless. Helping sell things to people that don't want them, and your choice of men is always shocking. Wasters, the lot of them. Seriously, what are you doing?"

I am speechless. I imagine my mouth agape and eyes like saucers. I don't know how to respond. I am saved by a knock at the door. It's Arthur.

"Oh, I'm sorry. Am I intruding?"

"No come in, Arthur, I was just giving our girl here some home truths in the hope that it would shake her up enough to not make the same mistakes again."

Arthur chuckles, "I think Ellie will welcome the distraction in that case. Don't mind Rose, she just loves you. We all do. That man didn't deserve you."

"Does everyone know my business?" I hide my face in my hands and feel like I want to climb inside myself.

"Only we know lovely. You're like family to us, we want to help. Angus knew that we would."

"Err, how does making me feel worse and having a go at me help? I just want to forget everything and run off somewhere never to return. If I go far enough away no one will know me."

Rose looks at me thoughtfully, she is clearly ruminating and considering her words carefully. Finally, she says, "A holiday is probably a good idea pet. Go away, get some sun on those bones. Rest and gather yourself then come home and start again refreshed and with a plan. You don't want to run away. Running away will help you escape your current woes, but it won't stop the same cycle happening again. You need to reboot yourself. Use this opportunity to do what you really want to do in your heart of hearts. That's what your Granny would have told you."

Arthur correctly senses that I have had enough and says cheerfully, "Hear, hear, Rose. Now, let's have some of this delicious cake before the tea goes cold."

I decide to walk back to Angus's. It's a long way but I need the space to think. Walking always helps calm my thoughts. All that Rose said was true and it is what my Granny would have said. Perhaps a little more delicately than Rose, but she would have got there in her way. I don't want to feel like this ever again. My usual way of doing things clearly isn't working so I need to do things differently. The problem is, I don't know where to start. I don't know how to start. I feel so lost and despite Rose, Arthur, Angus et al, I feel lonely. Really alone and lost.

Chapter Seven
Decisions

On my long walk after my 'Come to Jesus' session with Rose and Arthur, I decide that I can't think straight here in the shadow of my past life. Also, I'm homeless and I can't stay with Angus forever. Angus wouldn't mind to be fair, but Gemma is getting annoyed by my presence. I can see the stolen looks of, 'When are you going to get a life so that I can keep up my mission of becoming Mrs Angus Montague. She's really angling for it without saying it. Smart little operator is our Gemma. My guess is she will do anything Angus wants until they're married and then she'll call the shots. Expensive holidays will be booked, the credit card will be routinely obliterated, a small white snappy handbag dog will be purchased along with a blingy, white Land rover. The house will be overhauled to her taste and the open-all-hours sex shop will close for business. Oh Angus, you poor sod. I've seen it so many times. Relationships are all bollocks. I'm off them for good.

My Mum is calling me twice daily and texting me hourly virtually wetting herself at the thought of me returning home, but I would rather cut my own arm off and beat myself senseless with it. My parents are lovely, really lovely, but my Mum would try the patience of a saint in her pursuit to become a saint. She's very holy, very proper. She spends all her time away from the house at the church or doing church activities. I don't have anything against religion or her passion for it, but it's a bit exhausting when I go home as she expects me to join in. My dad is a pet, a long-suffering teddy bear of a man. He still works as a

Physiotherapist and has a practice at the house. I don't think he will ever stop working. He's really good at what he does and he loves it. He specialises in sports therapy. He has written for many medical journals and is a well sought-after speaker on the international circuit. His research has earned him many accolades globally and he guest lectures at all the top universities in Europe and America. I'm so proud of him. I'm super proud of mum too. She was a florist. She rose up the ranks in the local florist shop after she left school at sixteen, to eventually buying out the owner on her retirement from the business. She re-energised the place and made it a thriving enterprise. So much so that a large floristry chain made her an offer that she couldn't refuse and she sold the business five years ago. Since then, she has thrown herself into the community and the church. She is happy and content. Due to her business success, they are comfortable as they move into their twilight years.

When I was younger, I often wondered how they ever got together because they are so different. With the benefit of age and maturity, I see that they complement each other and that their base values are the same. They aren't drinkers, they have a small circle of close friends and they are happiest pottering around the house enjoying their hobbies or minutely planning culturally interesting holidays together. No beach holidays for my parents. Oh no. Last year they did a four-week Italian foodie tour. They visited three cookery schools and weaved in plenty of historical sights en-route. This year they are going to Croatia on a similar trip. Fair play to them I say. My brothers are less interested or happy about it. They and their bitchy wives frequently made snide remarks about spending our inheritance. If it were me, I would leave them nothing for their rudeness. I reckon they should enjoy life as much as they can. There will be plenty enough for us children and we're capable of looking after ourselves at this stage. Well, my brothers are and until recent events I was nicely on track.

My brothers, Eamon and Declan, are older than me by twelve and ten years, respectively. I was a happy accident. I like that because it's like I'm the free amaretto at the end of a meal or the unexpected fifty percent off at the till. I am joy. That's what my dad always says. I love Dad. Eamon, the eldest, boring accountant text me after the incident offering financial advice only. He doesn't do feelings, so it was a messy situation for him to talk to me about. I appreciated his message even though it was weirdly written. Declan and I were always close. He's a total messer, but the best fun ever. He lives in Australia much to my Mum's despair. He's an amazing specimen of a human being. Graduated medicine first in his class from Trinity. He trained as a surgeon in the top hospitals of the world and then joined doctors without borders. He travelled to the toughest places in the world and worked like a dog, trying to make a difference. He met his wife Libby through work. She is a human rights lawyer specialising in women's rights. Libby is from Australia, so when they decided to start a family they packed up their super hero jobs and settled in the suburbs of Sydney near Libby's family. They have an amazing quality of life there. I try to visit every other year. Declan does the same, so we end up seeing each other every year. It's not enough though. It's never enough. Declan wants to do a Skype call tomorrow morning at 9 am. It will be nighttime there. I'm looking forward to talking to him. He has a way of calming my mind and heart. He always did. I feel certain that a chat with him will steer me in the right direction.

People often ask me if I ever feel inferior compared to my brothers. The successful accountant and the superhero doctor. I hate the question because it means the questioner usually thinks that I am less than, in most cases. It's usually some ancient nosy aunt or one of my mum's church friends. The truth is, I know I'm brighter than both my brothers. I aced everything that I ever tried from maths to scuba diving. I chose marketing because I'm very creative. People think that it's fluffy. Maybe it is, but it suited me until now. Now it feels that I have given a large part of myself and wasted precious lifetime for something that really doesn't matter. At a basic level, I tart things up so that we can make people buy shit they don't need. That's not something you want to have on your gravestone… "She was amazing at putting lipstick on a pig." I know I'm having an existential crisis caused by recent events, but I really feel like I want to implode my life and start over again with a blank piece of paper. Maybe, I can. I want to. I just worry that my nature, my character and the inbuilt, learnt cycles of my behaviours will stop me from really breaking free. I'm so afraid that I will end up in this same place over and over again.

Chapter Eight
Declan – the Legend

I'm ready and waiting at my laptop the next morning at ten to nine. I'm showered and I've even blow dried my hair and put makeup on. I want to make an effort for Declan so that he doesn't worry about me too much. He's bang on time.

"Howdy gorgeous girl! I thought you might look like a shadow of your former self but you don't, you look great."

The plan worked, I think to myself. "Thanks, Declan. This is what no work does for you."

"Well, it suits you. I'm sorry to hear about your job and about the twat. You've had a really rough time. I'd love to fly over and lamp him for you. I always thought he was a bit smooth for my liking. Dirty bastard as it turns out. Angus told me that he implied we're all like that. About women and sex. Take it from me, we're not Ellie. He is just a prize twat and you're better off shot of him. Better now than three kids down the line. I know that doesn't help right now but in time you'll feel that it was a lucky escape."

This makes me smile wholeheartedly. "I would love to watch you thump him. A good older brother beating, but it's okay, I'm feeling less raw about it all now."

This isn't entirely true, but I am feeling a teeny bit better each day. "So, what are you doing tomorrow?" Declan asks.

"Um, laundry and a run maybe. Nothing much. Why? Do you need me to do something for you?"

Declan smiles widely, "Yes actually. I have booked you a flight to Sydney tomorrow. I need you to come over and spend some time here with me so that I can look after you properly."

I am flabbergasted. This is insane. I can't just up and go to Australia.

"Hello, Ellie, earth to Ellie! I can see the wheels churning in your mind. What's stopping you coming out to see your favourite brother for a bit? You might not get this chance of free time again. Just come Ellie. I love you and I miss you so much. I just want to give you a big cuddle and talk to you properly. Some makeup and a smile that doesn't reach your eyes does not convince me that you are okay. Remember I know you better than anyone."

I've started to sob as he speaks. Noiseless tears run continuously down my cheeks. I can't stop them coming. It's like a tap has been turned on that I can't turn off. I cover my face and sob and sob. I hate crying because I think it's weak and it makes me feel fragile, vulnerable and out of control. I especially hate crying in front of people. Even Declan. He speaks again, this time softly, "Ellie, it's okay, I know it feels like the end of the world but it's not. Come out to Aus. Get away from it all for a bit."

I breathe deeply in and out, wipe my tears and compose myself. A bit croaky and unconvincingly I thank Declan for the ticket and the lovely thought and accept the offer. I need to put myself in someone's hands right now as I am at sea and my brother is the best person in the world to hold me when I'm broken. I know that. Declan is mega excited that I'm coming and starts reaming off all the fun things that we can do. By the time we sign off his infectious excitement has rubbed off a little, but I'm still shaking with the emotional release and the shock of the trip. I need a strong cup of sweet tea and a biscuit to calm me down. Maybe two biscuits. Hell, maybe half the packet!

Declan told me to check my email for the flight details. I am amazed and delighted that he has booked me first class all the way. I've never flown first in my life. Business class to London with work is the best I've managed. It's a long journey. I leave Dublin at ten at night and fly to Dubai. I have a short wait and then connect for a flight to Sydney. The total journey time is about twenty-three hours. I'll leave

Dublin on Tuesday and arrive at six in the morning on Thursday in Australia. When I did it before, I went via London and in economy. Declan said that he'll pick me from the airport before going to work. Now that I see the flight details in black and white, I am getting really excited. I love Sydney and obviously can't wait to spend time with my brother and his family. His wife Libby is great and my nieces are sweeties. Perhaps this change of scene is exactly what I need.

Oh, Lordy, I need to get my skates on. I get a horrible sinking feeling as I realise that all my stuff is at the flat. At HIS flat, The Bastard's flat. I glance at my watch, which tells me that it's just after nine. I still have my key and he'll be at work. Mhmm, I do need to rescue my belongings at some stage. I didn't think it would be today but I guess it has to be. It's that or drip into my settlement from work. I don't want to misuse it as it's my only income at the moment so I'll need to revisit the scene of the crime and liberate my belongings.

I dress in all black, joggers, tee and hat. It's not deliberate but I look like I'm about to do a bank heist, I feel like a thief but I'm just going to get my own things back. I tell myself that it's absolutely fine. I guess I could text him to tell him but that would mean contacting him and I don't really want to do that. So I don't. I head to the flat in my beloved red Mini Cooper. I love this car. I saved and saved to buy it and bought it new paying for it outright. I clean it by hand every Saturday morning at the local carwash where they have hoses and industrial vacuums for two euro per half hour. My car air freshener is a fancy, fresh cotton Yankee Candle one because my little car deserves to smell gorgeous. It's like perfume for le car. I've decided to park out the front of the building in a service-parking stop. I ask the concierge to watch the car while I run up and chuck stuff quickly in black plastic bags. Thankfully it's not Bill. It's someone new. As I ride the lift up clutching my bin bags, it feels very weird to be back here after what happened. I open my old, front door and take a deep breath before going in. It's quiet and still. There's no one here, just me. A sudden rush of sadness and homesickness washes over me like someone's poured a bucket of warm water over my head. I've lost so much more than my job and my boyfriend. I've also lost my home and the future that I imagined for myself. At this moment, the loss feels crushing and overwhelming. Why me? I'm a good person, what have I done to deserve this? I close my eyes and breathe deeply to centre myself again, to regain control of my emotions. I need to just get this done quickly and get the hell out of here.

I enter my bedroom, our bedroom. It smells of him. The bed has been made. The whole place is tidier than I expected and to my huge relief there are no signs of another woman. I hadn't realised that this had been concerning me until now. I suppose it was a worry that he would just move on immediately to someone else. I don't think my ego could have taken that knock. My things are exactly as I left them, including the book I was reading overturned by my side of the bed, and my pyjamas under the pillow. This is a little touching, like he doesn't want it to be over, maybe he thinks it is fixable. I physically shake myself for having such thoughts. I dump my underwear and clothes in two bin bags and then use a separate one for toiletries. The last bag is for miscellaneous things like books, DVD's, my yoga stuff, expensive cooking herbs I bought and my favourite mugs. When I've bagged up everything; it equals seven large bin bags. What a sad indictment of my life. As I take a last lingering walk around the place, I notice my mail has been neatly piled up. I shove this in the miscellaneous bag for later. I dislodge the door key from my key ring and place it on the island unit. Fitting, I think, given that was the scene of the crime. With one last, deep breath, I gather up my bags and hit the road.

Bill is back when I get downstairs. He kindly helps me to load up the car. He is very red in the face and clearly embarrassed.

"I'm so sorry about what happened. I wanted to warn you before you went upstairs that he had women up there, but I didn't know how and thought I'd get in trouble. You have always been so nice to me. I can tell that you are a good person. He doesn't deserve you, you're better than him. But if it makes you feel any better, since that day, he looks awful. He seems really depressed and has let his appearance go completely. He's not even bothering to shave. It looks like he has a lot of regrets."

This little monologue is unexpected so I am a bit taken aback. I manage a "Thank you" and a "Don't worry about it" before giving him an awkward and probably inappropriate hug in lieu of knowing what to do.

Back in the security of my little car, I take stock of how I'm feeling. My heart is racing a mile a minute. The adrenaline probably. I am comforted somewhat that Alex is regretful and that he hasn't jumped straight into bed with someone else, but I don't want him back. I don't want that life back. I want a new, better life. I have no idea what it'll be like or how I'll achieve it but the confidence of knowing that I am moving towards it with each small step makes me feel proud of myself. Goodbye, swanky penthouse flat. Goodbye, Alex.

Chapter Nine
The Journey, Not the Destination

Whatever I do next, I need to make enough money to fly like this all the time. First class flying is so awesome. I'm sure the air stewards can spot first timers a mile off. I am trying to be cool and collected but I reckon I look like a child on Christmas morning instead.

"Can I offer you a refreshment madam? I have some orange juice or champagne?"

Is there any doubt about my answer? Nope!

"Champagne please!" It's fizzy and delicious and it's in a real glass, glass. Not like the plastic glasses in economy. I stare about the cabin-watching people as they come in. There are lots of older gentlemen wearing Ralph Lauren or similar. Some have their wives with them, but most are solo. There are two banker looking types and a few sneaker and hoodie clad cool looking forty somethings. Maybe marketing or techy types. One family with two teenage kids and a girl about my age in a really comfy looking tracksuit and uggs. She has her hair piled up and goes about settling in with the ease or someone who travels a lot. When she's settled, she takes out her laptop and types furiously. I wish I'd dressed like that but I thought I should make an effort to look halfway decent in first. Stupid really. Although I do look smart in my tight jeans, crisp white shirt and navy blazer. Pearls for jewellery and a leopard print scarf. Maybe one of these billionaires will take a shine to me. Joking! Obviously.

I watch three movies and a TV series. One of them, a comedy, is so funny that I actually laugh out loud. The couple across from me shoot me dirty looks, but I can't help it. It's hilarious. I adore inane comedy. It's my guilty secret. People always expect me to have a much more cultured taste in film but my favourite movie ever is American Pie! I love the menu card and that I can choose. On this first leg of the journey, lunch is an assortment of canapés hot and cold, daube of beef with seasonal vegetables and a Crème caramel for dessert with tea or coffee. Yummy! Service is all fresh white linen and silverware with more wine and champagne. I feel truly spoiled rotten, especially when I'm tucked in to my fully flat bed with a fleece blanket, pillows, slippers and a glass of wine watching a movie. Life is good. Thank you Declan! The girl in the tracksuit and uggs works solidly throughout the flight. She looks pretty intense. I might have been like that last week. I don't want to be her again.

When I finally land in Sydney, I'm pretty tired and feeling sweaty from a long journey. I could really do with a shower and a stretch. A quick ten-minute sun salutation yoga session should put me right. Declan is waiting in arrivals. Two coffees in hand and grinning from ear to ear. What a gorgeous, lovely legend he is. I race my trolley to him and nearly spill the coffee in my bear embrace. He hugs me back with the same love. I'm so glad to be here with my big brother. I feel like the world is right and that things are getting better all the time.

Chapter Ten
Australia

After many late-night chats with Declan over a bottle or two of wine and days filled with sun and giggles with my nieces, I am feeling loved, centred and whole again. This trip was such a good idea. Initially I felt like it was running away, but really it was running back to myself. After a two weeks stay with Declan and his gorgeous family, I decide that I need a bit of space so I blow a fortune on a stunning wellness retreat and organise a hire car to get me there.

Namaste, Lodge, the retreat centre is stunningly beautiful. It sits on a large lagoon and little wooden lodges discreetly sit in the woods by the water's edge. The lodges are incredible. I have two living areas, one inside and one on a huge deck overlooking the still water. I have a two person-floating bath in my bedroom as well as a rain shower in the bathroom. I even have my own hammock in a tree by the deck. It is an eco-retreat, therefore there is local wood everywhere and gorgeous organic fabrics and toiletries. This really is such an unbelievable treat. Many a time I would read my yoga magazines and drool over the retreats in far-flung places. Never did I think I would get to go to one. I have signed up for the five-day retreat. I have Hatha Flow Yoga at 7 am for an hour and a half followed by a breakfast of juices, food and cereals. I then have meditation class followed by a treatment. I have free time in the afternoon. The second yoga class of the day is at 6.30 p.m. and this is a restorative yoga class. Dinner follows this and then there is an optional candlelight yoga and meditation class at 10.30 p.m. for anyone still awake. As soon as I walked into the reception, I felt all the tension drifting away. This place is pure magic. I'm so excited to jump into my itinerary.

I haven't done much yoga this last while with all the drama, so as I wait on my mat at 6.55 am on day one I am a little apprehensive that I'll be out of my depth. I sneak a few looks around the class to assess the level of my classmates. There are eight of us. Six women and two men. Two hot men actually. Very hot men. One looks quite moody and introverted. He has serious bed hair and looks like he's not happy to be up and exercising at this time of the morning. He's very cute though. The other guy is full on serious yogi. He's already limbering up and has his top off thus showing off his impressive physique. He looks like a gymnast or something. I didn't really expect any men and the sight of two attractive ones has turned my head. I must concentrate. I must not be distracted by the hot guys! Maybe just one more sneaky look! Hahahaha. The women in the group are made up of two older ladies, clearly friends away together, a petite Asian girl with beautiful long, black hair down to her waist, a mega hippy chick with dreadlocks, cool tattoos and piercings, and two other normal looking girls about my age. They all look friendly enough but you never know at these retreats. People can be quite weird when thrown together like this. I think it heightens all character traits so you can end up having some extreme encounters. I picked this one because it's deliberately not too group oriented. We don't have to eat together and there is a lot of individual free time.

Our teacher breezes in with a flow of cool air.

"Good morning to all you beautiful people, how lucky are we to be alive today and in this incredible place together? My name is Sasha, and I will be taking your morning yoga class for the duration of your stay. We will hopefully awaken your body and mind and push you to the next level of flexibility and relaxation. For all the flows and positions, I will give variations so that you can decide how far to push yourselves. There is no competition in Yoga. We move at our own pace, so be kind and gentle with yourself and try to listen to what your body is telling you when it's tight or sore or flying. Okay, your registration forms tell me that we have no injuries but if anyone has a tinge in class or needs me at all, please raise your hand, and I will be straight over. Okay beautiful people, let's start in the seated position."

Yippee! We're off! I roll my head to the left and right and breathe deeply. I know this session will be tough, since my body is stiff with inactivity and the tension of the last few weeks. I breathe deeply letting myself surrender to the instructions. As the flows get faster and more challenging, I find myself out of breath and working up a sweat. It just shows that you lose fitness quicker than you gain it. Its hard work but I love it.

Sasha is a great teacher. She seems to have quickly understood everyone's baseline and she works her way around us all making small adjustments to our positions. I love when teachers do this and you can immediately feel the difference. She pushes my lower back in a backwards bend. It nearly takes my breath away but I gain a much deeper stretch and it feels amazing. I'm getting really tired and all my muscles are hot, I'm at the point of no more when Sasha tells us to get into shavasana. This is a relaxation pose at the end of a class. It is the most incredible feeling to just let go of all your effort, exhaustion and stress and let the floor take the weight. It honestly feels like you are floating, like you are a being of air. I could fall asleep here, but after a long-guided rest Sasha gets us to sit up and wishes us Namaste. Class one was awesome. Now for a yummy breakfast. I have opted to have breakfast on my sun deck. When I arrive back at my pad, I find that the food fairies have been and there is a perfect feast laid out on the outdoor table. Dainty pastries, jams, fruit salad, porridge, various breads, cheeses, ham. Fresh squeezed orange juice and tea will wash it all down. This is like a feast for four people but I will darn well give it a go. This might possibly be my idea of heaven. Sitting here in nature, listening to the birds, gazing out on the water, sun on my face, eating delicious food. I am so relaxed, happy and contented. Heaven. Definitely heaven.

Chapter Eleven
The Wellness Retreat

The days continue in this manner. Brilliant classes, amazing treatments and lush food. I am positively glowing with health and happiness. This place is wonderful. As I walk back to my lodge from a Lomilomi massage, I meet the mega buff guy and the petite Asian girl. Brad and Nina it turns out. Brad is clearly checking me out. He does this to all women between the ages of 16 and 40, I have noticed. I suspect he's a major player. He smiles, a very white, winning smile, "Hey, it's Ellie isn't it? Nina and I were just saying that we should all meet for a drink tonight in the bar. It's a nice group. It would be cool to get to know everyone better. What do you think?"

In my head I'm like, no fucking way. I'm here to be by myself and I'm having a great time in my own company. I have plenty of friends so am not looking to make any more. But I politely say, "That sounds like a great idea. Shall we meet after dinner?"

I am forever polite. It's been drilled into me by my mother and now I can never say no to people. It's a major frustration of mine. Thanks Mum! I continue on to my room. Annoyingly the encounter has ruffled my previous serene mood and I'm now dreading later. Uff! I know it's only drinks, but I really don't want to speak to anyone right now. I have a bad feeling about it. I feel the storm clouds gathering around me. But bloody hell Ellie, if you can't even face a drink with a group of nice, like-minded people, you are not ready to go back to the real world. I know I need to just suck it up. What is wrong with me!

I end up having dinner with Freda and Nell, the two older ladies and the two girls my age, Nadia and Simone. We actually have a nice time after we get over the awkwardness of the initial small talk. Nadia is from London and Simone is from Brisbane. The three of us all work in marketing and like a lot of the same things, so the conversation flows easily. After dinner we are joined by the rest of the group and we all stand at the bar. I'm on water as I am not drinking on this retreat. I'm not spending a fortune at a wellness retreat to get completely lashed and ruin all my good work. Brad is working the crowd. I think he's evaluating how many women he can sleep with in the group. I hope I have every barrier up as I could do without an awkwardly rejected advance this week. I think I'm okay though, as he currently has his hand on the small of Nina's back while holding Nadia's hand and complimenting her yoga style. I kind-of want to vomit in my mouth. My ex probably collects women like this too. Bastard!

My thoughts are broken my Ms Hippy Dippy as she envelopes me in a hug. She reeks of heady incense sticks. I'm all about the personal space so this unexpected embrace from a stranger throws me and I giggle nervously. "Ellie, you are a beautiful soul. I felt your incredible energy as soon as I set eyes upon you. You must allow the world to see and hear your truth. You could be a beacon of light for the world, if you would just let yourself shine."

As she rabbits on, she comes closer and closer towards me. I retreat as she does this until I'm against a wall and she's pretty much on top of me. She is clearly bat crazy and probably mega high. Wow, how normal am I! I just smile nervously and let her go on and on. Out of the corner of my eye I notice the bed hair guy looking at the scene smiling, with a lot of amusement in his eyes. He mouths, "Are you okay?"

I roll my eyes covertly so that mad mamma doesn't see. He excuses himself from his conversations with Freda and Nell and makes his way over to us.

"Astrid."

"Yes, Ben?"

"I think I just saw a shooting star over there that you might fancy taking a look at."

"OMG really, did it land in the lagoon? I bet it did. I think that lagoon is magical. Perhaps is power comes from shooting stars. Wow, thanks, Ben, I'm going to go and count the ripples on the water." She continues to mumble to herself as she rushes off into the darkness to investigate.

I laugh out loud. A laugh of relief. "Thank you very much. That was getting weird and intense." He laughs too. It's a warm, comfortable laugh, "Yeah, I had a similar encounter yesterday, so I recognised your deer in a headlight look and thought I should rescue you. She's harmless, really. Just a bit mental. You get all sorts of people at these things."

"It sounds like you go on them a lot?" I question.

"Yes, well it's part of my work. I'm a journalist specialising in health and wellbeing." I'm visibly impressed.

"Wow! That sounds like a cool job. How does one get into that? It's not exactly a typical career day answer." He goes on to tell me that he trained as a doctor. After graduating he specialised in oncology. "I had this idealised dream of helping to cure cancer, but obviously it's a lot more complex than that. I lost so many patients. People in the prime of life, children, people not ready to go. I stopped counting how many. It affected me. Much more than I had anticipated. With every death I felt that I had failed. It wasn't rational I know, but I had become depressed. Then sadly my Dad became ill and he became one of my patients. His death was the last straw for me. After he died, I took an extended leave on health grounds and then I never went back. I kind of fell into this writing lark, and pleasantly found that I was rather good at it and enjoyed it. It's grown over the years and now I'm quite well known in the field and get to come to dream locations like this one."

He stops talking, catches my eye and looks embarrassed. He even goes a bit red in the cheeks and on his neck. It makes him look boy-like and adorable as he reddens, looks at the ground and shuffles his shoes. I put him out of his misery.

"I'm so sorry for your loss. I can't imagine how hard it was to watch and treat your Dad knowing the detail of what was going on. I'm sure your Dad would be really proud of the way your life turned out."

He looks up and gives a smile of thanks, with the softest of looks from his mellow brown eyes. He really is gorgeous. And a doctor. Well ex doctor who is into wellness and yoga. He can't be real. Perhaps he's a mirage.

"As I've embarrassingly unburdened myself, what's your story? Why are you here?"

I have a sudden feeling of panic. I don't want to tell this gorgeous stranger that I'm a total fuck up with no job, a cheating boyfriend and no future plans. Shit! What do I say? I think he must sense my panic. He helpfully says, "I'm sorry, that's a heavy question. Let's start with where you're from as that lovely accent is not Australian."

He thinks my accent is lovely…swoon. We spend the evening chatting easily about everything from horrible, Granny-knitted Christmas jumpers to our taste in music. We have lots in common and he's a pleasure to be with. As the bar music turns of and it's turning in time, I realise that I am smitten. I don't want to go to bed. I want to talk to him all night long. But he clearly doesn't share my feelings as he jumps up when the music stops. "Oh wow, is that the time? It's so late and we're the last ones here. I didn't even hear the others leave. We should head back too otherwise we'll be useless for Sasha in the morning."

"Oh, yes, absolutely." I manage. A little too fake enthusiastically.

We walk along the dimly lit pathway around the lagoon in silence. It's not an awkward silence, but I can't help wishing he'd take my hand. He doesn't, but he does reach over and kiss my cheek when we say goodnight at my lodge. He smells of musk. Deep musky loveliness. As he stands back, he looks at me with those same soft eyes that I saw earlier when we talked about his Dad. For a moment I'm certain that he's going to kiss me. Properly this time. But then he quickly walks off mumbling a goodbye and waving behind him. I'm left staring after him wondering if the moment had ever happened. Perhaps my radar for when a man likes me is all off kilter after recent events. I've probably made a complete dope of myself by flirting with him and he didn't know how to extract himself from the situation. I'm so stupid. Why would a gorgeous, nice man be interested in me? Clearly and definitely not. I think it's best if I stick to my original plan of a reclusive, individual retreat and avoid human contact when at all possible. To this end, I'll order breakfast to my room tomorrow morning to avoid an awkward breakfast meeting. As I go to bed, I find it hard to sleep as my brain is in overdrive. I feel silly and disappointed and unsettled. I'm so cross. I came here to heal and enjoy my own company and I have my head turned by the first good-looking guy I meet. For God's sake! What is wrong with me!

In the morning, I awake full of resolve to enjoy my day. The sun rising on the lagoon is just gorgeous and the breakfast spread is utterly yummy. I have time for a read in the hammock before the first yoga class of the day. I time my arrival at yoga, so that I will be the last. So that I can slip silently and unnoticed in the back. I do this and take up position in a row of my own at the back. Everyone is already in seated position and Sasha is starting, so no one turns to me. Thank goodness. I give myself fully to the session. I push and pull my body further and harder than I ever have before. I feel like a warrior. I rise early from the final shavasana and slip out quietly. I run back to my lodge, expelling any pent-up emotions and throw myself into my hammock to rest. I fall asleep here and am only awoken by the movements of the maid in to clean and service the room. I never nap. I always have such trouble sleeping. I must have totally wiped myself in the yoga session. I have missed the mediation session, and have only ten minutes until my daily treatment. I'll have to run to get to the treatment rooms. It's so unlike me.

“Morning, Mona,” I say to my therapist.

“I’m sorry I’m a little late, but I fell asleep after a yoga session and woke with a bit of a start. I never nap like that. I don’t know what’s up with me.”

Mona regards me gently. She ushers me to sit down and makes me a cup of herbal tea. Camomile, which I love. “Ellie, you are very tired. Exhausted actually. This is not surprising given what you told me about your recent life events. I think you have been efficiently holding it all together, but now you are allowing your body to relax and it wants too, rather it needs to rest. You need to listen to your body, Ellie. Seriously. I am worried about you. Please promise me that you will rest the next few weeks and then thereafter when you get home. You need to mind yourself.” I’m a bit taken aback by her candour and clarity. I suspect that she is right. I’m not good at minding myself. I’m not good at resting. When I am relaxing, I’m making lists and tidying and planning. I need to learn how to just stop and do nothing. I know I do. I have friends that can lie in bed half the day, but even with the worst hangover I have to get up and get busy. I guess I am a busy fool.

Mona gives me a restorative aromatherapy massage and instructs me to go straight for a nap which I do. Lying under the fresh, crisp, white linen sheets I feel so relaxed that I can barely feel my limbs. Mona did an amazing job. She instructed me to not set my alarm. I can’t remember ever not setting my alarm, but I do as she told me and drift contentedly off to sleep.

Chapter Twelve
Ben

After an amazing sleep, I am woken by the waiter setting up my dinner on the deck area. I have slept for seven hours! I can't believe it. I still feel tired though and my body aches but I feel good, snugly. On my avoidance trip I ordered dinner to my room last night. It was a fortuitous choice, given my groggy mood and bed head appearance. I really don't want to do small talk. I don't want to face Ben either. Dinner is yummy. Goat cheese salad with pine nuts, lamb tagine followed by seasonal fruits Pana Cotta. I make myself a warming peppermint tea to wash it all down and then lounge in my hammock. I must get a house with a garden when I go home so that I can have a hammock. They really are so relaxing. I think it's because your body is fully supported and encased.

I need to unleash myself from the cocoon of my room for the evening yoga session. I'm nervous to see Ben, but I don't want to miss the session, as it is a candlelight restorative class tonight with a guided meditation at the end. It will be lovely to do that and then go straight to sleep. So I pluck up the courage, shower, dress and head to class. I arrive late again and sneak into the back. Sasha notices and gives me a slight nod and smile in acknowledgement. The class is absolutely yummy. By the end I am totally relaxed and sleepy. Just as I did this morning, I get up early from the shavasana and leave unnoticed. Back at my lodge I think a hot drink and a bath are in order. I feel like being decadent and really spoiling myself so I order a hot chocolate with cream and marshmallows. It comes with just made, warm almond cookies. I think I'm actually in heaven. As I linger in a hot bubble bath and sip my drink with my eyes closed in bliss. I jump with a start at the sound of something jabbing and shrill. What the hell was that? I listen out for it, but nothing. I'm about to drip back under the water when there it is again. I realise it's the doorbell. Duh, stupid me. I place my drink down carefully and grab a towel. I drape it around myself a pad damply to the door where I peer out the peephole. Nothing. I check again. Nothing. I open the door and lean out looking all around. The place is deserted with no one in sight. Maybe it was housekeeping or the waiter forget something when he came with my hot chocolate. Weird. Back in my room, I look sadly at my bath. I can't get back in now as the moment has passed, time to dress for bed. As I tidy up before bed and turn the lights off, I notice something on the mat by the front door. A hotel envelope. Maybe it's the room service bill. I lift it and bring it to bed with me. Ellie is written on the front. That's a bit informal for a hotel. It's usually Ms. But it's not from the hotel, it's a note from Ben. OMG, WTF! Why is he sending me a note? It reads…

"Dear, Ellie, I'm sorry if I made you feel awkward last night. It was the last thing I wanted to do as I think you are rather lovely. Ben x"

I wasn't expecting that. He thinks I am rather lovely. My cheeks blush despite myself and my heart races at the thought of his soft eyes. He likes me. Do I want a holiday romance though? I'm going home in a few days, do I need that possible heartbreak on top of everything I've been through. Probably not. But oh! Those eyes and that smile. I curl up to go to sleep, happy and excited for tomorrow. I haven't felt this way in a long time.

Instead of slouching into the back of the class I set my alarm early to make sure I look good and so that I can grab herbal tea before class in the hope of catching Ben. When I get to the breakfast room most people are already there. There's a chorus of "What happened to you yesterday?" to which I blush and mumble something about feeling off colour. Ben is by the herbal tea station smiling broadly. "Morning, Ellie. You look…" He seems to be clutching for words.

"Lovely?" I say with a cheeky raised eyebrow and a smile. I can't believe myself. I'm flirting already. He laughs.

"Yes, lovely. You look lovely."

Gesturing to the tea he says, "Can I interest you in a lemon and ginger infusion tea?"

"How did you know my morning tea?"

He smiles and looks down. Shyly he says that he'd noticed on the first morning. So, he's been watching me. How did I not register that! I guess my mind was elsewhere. The attentiveness is very nice and as we all head to the first yoga class of the day, Ben and I set up beside each other. I'm determined not to be distracted by him but it's hard not to steal glances. He's a very good yogi. Strong and focussed in his movement. I'm more catlike. Always rocking and tweaking postures, in perpetual motion. Like my mind I guess, constantly going. After class we enjoy a long leisurely breakfast and then he asks me if I'd like to go for a walk around the lagoon. I would like that, so I agree. We retreat to our rooms to refresh up and I take a few minutes lying on my bed to close my eyes and smile. To enjoy the happy feeling that you get when you meet someone you like. When you know they like you back and you can't wait to spend more time together.

After spending the day together, dinner, drinks and talking late into the night, the kiss at my door is natural and wonderful. I've been waiting to be kissed all day. Perhaps he's kept me waiting deliberately so that I am like putty in his hands. We kiss and kiss for ages. It's like the kisses of teenagers. Long, passionate and not hurried. Kissing for kissing. Not as a prelude to anything else. I feel this in his kiss. That there will be no more than this tonight and I'm content with that. I'm not ready for more. Maybe he knows, maybe he isn't ready either. Either way, I'm loving being held and kissed.

The days roll on blissfully, until it's the final evening. Ben has arranged a surprise. I am to be ready at seven thirty. At seven fifteen I am ready and waiting. I have plucked, waxed, brushed, made up and beautified myself as much as humanly possible. Thank goodness I brought an appropriate dress with me. It's a gorgeous, dark floral, long flowing chiffon dress. I impulse bought it in Sydney and stuffed it in my bag at the last moment. I have curled the ends of my hair and had my makeup done in the spa. That may have been a step too far but I feel really special. I have fallen hard for Ben. In only a few short days I am besotted. I don't want to leave Australia without him, but I know I will have to. I want tonight to be as perfect as it can be.

Bang on seven thirty, there is an upbeat knock at the door. I open it to find a yummy Ben in linen trousers and shirt. His shirt is teasingly opened three buttons giving a hint of that tanned, toned yogi chest. He looks edible. He doesn't say anything, just smiles broadly with his eyes alight in the darkness. After what feels like forever, he takes my hand and pulls me to him. Nuzzles into my neck breathing me in and whispers, "You look sensational."

I cup his face and kiss him intently. We stumble backwards into my room, kicking the door closed. My beautiful dress is off in seconds along with his shirt. Somehow, we navigate ourselves to my bed and I pull him down on top of me. I have never wanted a man more. I feel like my body is about to explode. Every touch of his sends shivers through my entire being. He feels the same. I can feel it. Emotionally and physically we are matching each other, pushing each other onwards into heights of euphoria. It doesn't last long the first time because we are dying for each other and we explode and collide quickly and satisfyingly. Ben had planned a romantic dinner on the banks of the lagoon but following our newfound intimacy neither of us want to be around other people so we get the catering team to setup the dinner on my deck instead. There we enjoy a delicious five-course feast, champagne and incredible sex breaks between courses. I think this might be the best night of my life. I have never felt more alive, more loved, more sexy, more content.

At some point we must have fallen asleep as I am woken annoyingly by my phone alarm beeping. I set it yesterday afternoon so that I got up in time to travel to the airport. I feel around for Ben in the bed, but he is not there. He's gone. I grip the cover tightly around me and cry. Deep, body-racking tears for a love found and lost. I get ready in a sad, tearful daze. Before leaving the room, I survey it one last time. It's such a beautiful space. What an amazing week I've had here. Remnants of dinner and an extreme night of passion are evident everywhere. The cleaners will be surprised although I'm sure it's not something that they haven't seen before. My reflective mood is broken by a light knock at the door. Maybe it's Ben? My heart beats faster as I hopefully open it. My stomach lurches to the floor. It's not Ben, it's the porter for my bags. I follow him silently to reception and checkout. The porter pulls my car round to the front door and loads my bags in the back before handing me my keys. I'm just thanking him when I hear "Ellie" behind me. It's Ben. He looks frantic and perplexed.

"I didn't realise that you were leaving so early. I went to get your herbal tea and some flowers. When I got back and saw that you had gone, I couldn't believe it. I'm so glad I caught you." I cry and smile and hug him all at the same time. Squashing the newly picked flowers in his hand.

"I thought you left. I thought maybe you regretted it. I thought…" He doesn't let me finish. He put the tea and flowers aside and cups my face in his hands. Looking at me softly, but intensely he says, "Ellie, last night was amazing. Meeting you has been wonderful. My only regret is that you are leaving."

He pauses as if debating what to say in his head.

"Stay. I want you to stay." I'm floored. I must look it as he removes his hands and retreats a little. I'm speechless and confused so all that comes out is, "I can't. I need to go home. My flight is booked."

He looks so sad. I feel so sad. I need to get going if I'm going to make my flight but how can we leave it like this. Ben recovers himself and as if reading my mind says, "You need to get going. This isn't the last conversation that we're going to have. I was rash just blurting out for you to stay. Don't mind me. Let me know when you get safely at the airport."

He gets me into the car and pops the flowers on the passenger seat and the tea in the cup holder before coming back around to my side and kissing me long and hard. "This is not the end Ellie. It's just the beginning for me." This is said like a question.

"Me too. I've really fallen for you I'm afraid." He smiles widely.

"Don't be afraid. Be excited. Let's try to focus on the joy not the distance." I nod. He is right. Smart, lovely and gorgeous. As I drive and sip the tea, Ben made for me I think to myself, who knew I'd go to Australia to get over a nasty breakup and losing my job and come back with a new (sort of) boyfriend. Someone who could be that elusive soul connect. Someone I'm mad about already. It's great but why can't my life be easy. He lives on the other side of the world! I don't half make things difficult for myself. I'm a nightmare. I can just imagine Angus rolling his eyes when he finds out!

Chapter Twelve
The House

On my return to Ireland I have no choice but to stay with Mum and Dad. It was kind of them to let me and for a few weeks it was nice because we were all on our best behaviour and it was lovely to be spoiled for a while. Dad and I had the funniest chats and I helped him in his practice. Mum cooked all my favourite food while also reorganising my wardrobe and persuading me to try a new hairstyle. Shorter and choppier. She was right – she usually is, although I will never admit that to her!

After a month I was ready to go though. Mum was starting to meddle too much. She kept trying to set me up with random people's sons. She also kept emailing me job suggestions and was forever getting me to help at the church. She meant well but it was frustrating and stifling. All the time I was there I was hatching a plan. I was planning for my next chapter. A proper adventure.

When my Granny passed away, I was named as the benefactor of a house in Donegal. The solicitor had no specific details of the property and said that he would have to liaise with a colleague in Donegal to get to the bottom of it. My Mum convinced me that is was just an old barn structure that sat at the bottom of someone's garden, where my Granny used to grow vegetables and herbs. I had totally forgotten about it until I received a call from her solicitor when I was with Declan in Sydney. It turned out that Granny did own a house in Donegal and it was quite a substantial sized house. My Mum still warned me that it would be derelict, and rat infested in the back end of nowhere most likely but nevertheless I felt excited about it and grateful to Granny for thinking of me. While with Declan, an idea started to form in my mind about refurbishing the house and turning it into a yoga school. It is something that I have always secretly dreamed of doing. With this inheritance and the money from work I might just be in a position to make my dream come true. Declan was tough on me and made me do a five-year business plan while I was with him. It was great because it focused my mind and made me realise that it might just be possible!

Donegal has such fond memories for me. My parents were teachers, so we used to go up there in the summer for six weeks. It was six weeks of playing outside, eating frcsh homemade food, going to the beach, enjoying long walks in the hills and eating lots of really hearty food in local pubs and restaurants. There is a particular smell in Donegal, it's a mix of turf, cut grass, sea and salt. There is a certain place on the way into the village where we stayed, where that smell would hit you and you felt, "I'm here. I have arrived." So I was quite looking forward to going back to Donegal but also apprehensive in case that feeling wasn't there anymore, but luckily as soon as I started to drive through the lush green mountains I realised that the feeling was exactly the same. It's just so ruggedly, un-spoilt and largely uninhabited. It's so easy to imagine that you are the only person in the world.

As nice as it was to be here, it wasn't a holiday and I was nervous about seeing the house for the first time. I still can't believe that Granny left it to me. Nobody in the family even knew about the house. We knew the story of how her Mum, my great Granny had fallen in love, run away from home and eloped with the local baker's son. She was subsequently disowned by her wealthy, land owning family. What we didn't know was that after she died, my Granny, as the last surviving member of the family inherited the original house that her mother had fled from. Granny never told anyone, so when it showed up in the will it was a big shock to all. I was a little surprised that my relatives weren't more perplexed by it or jealous that it had been left to me, but on seeing it I realised why. It was in a rather ramshackle state and it was in the middle of nowhere, which would make access really difficult for my builders and my students!

On first viewing, I had to scrutinise the map. I was like, 'Where is it?' I couldn't see anything. After scanning the area for five minutes, I finally spotted a chimney, just poking out above some very tall and dense trees. The house was totally enveloped in shrubbery, but the location and aspect of the house was just beautiful. It looks out over a lake in the middle of the mountains. It is so serene, peaceful and isolated. It's pretty spectacular really. It's a potentially perfect place for a yoga school and it's mine! All mine. I suddenly feel a huge sense of calm. It's as though I have come home and that everything is falling into place. I take a moment and look up in the sky, "Thank you, Granny. You clever old sausage. Thank you for giving me this chance, for putting me on the right path. I won't let you down. Love you so much. How I wish you were here with me now."

Maybe deep inside I thought it might be in the middle of nowhere because I rented a big four by four car at the airport. Normally, I'd be more of a hot hatch kind of girl. The big beast of a car makes it easier for me to cross the dirt track slash bog to get to the house. It feels like a proper off-road adventure. Perhaps I can make this part of my experience I think bleakly. On my arrival outside, where the house should be, I see that I'm going to have to wrestle my way through some serious shrubbery. If I'd been sensible, I would have brought hedge cutters or something, but no I'm here with my handbag only. Such an idiot! I should have known when I picked the key up from the solicitor. He refused to come and show me the property and suggested I sold it for the land and never went near the place at all. I don't think I've met a more unhelpful, miserable person. Anyway, let's try see to the matter at hand. How am I going to get through these bushes to the front door? Aha. I spot a sturdy looking branch lying on the ground and use it to attack the scrubs like a machete. Leaves and branches are flying everything and it's tiring work, but I'm loving it. I'm imagining The Bastard and venting all my repressed anger. It's great therapy!

When I eventually get to see the house, it is substantial and in better condition than I expected. The lock turns easily in the door and I get my torch out at the ready. The car came with a roadside emergency kit, which included the torch luckily. Another thing I should have thought of but didn't! Inside it is really dark as there are big heavy shutters and they are all closed and obviously the electricity is switched off. It smells of damp and age and something else that I can't quite put my finger on. It's not an unpleasant smell, but it is stifling. I quickly decide to open the shutters so I take my trusty torch room to room and open up the shutters and the windows. As I open everything up, I feel like I'm giving rebirth to the house, opening her up again. It is a joyous feeling. As I open the shutters, I deliberately don't take in the rooms, I want to do that slowly, so I work diligently at my task. Once I have everything open, I go back down to the front door again so that I can see everything from the front to the back. Wow, there is a lot of work to do! I'm not sure my budget is going to go that far here! Hey ho! That's tomorrow's problem. The hallway is very spacious. Straight opposite the front door there is a staircase that snakes up in a curve with a lovely wooden banister which I imagine might be shiny if polished. The stairs are bare but you can see where the tread of the carpet used to be. The walls are covered in a faint yellow wallpaper with little violet flowers on it. It's worn and torn in places so it will need taken down and replaced or painted. That's a shame because it's pretty. I dread to think what the walls are like underneath. To the left there's a room which I imagine was a drawing room. It has two windows at the front which overlook the lake and then another window to the side. You can barely see anything through them because of the overgrown garden. When it's all cleared this will be a lovely, bright, sunny room with a stunning view. The ceiling has old original cornicing which looks quite intact. There is even a ceiling rose. The ceilings are high giving a great sense of space. Walking back across the hall, I go into a room on the right. It is a mirror image of the room on the left. Again, another lovely room. Coming back out of the room, I go down a hall that runs under the staircase. There is smaller room to the left. It might have been a library or office maybe. There's a huge mirror in the corner covered in dust. It's ornate with cherubs and flowers around the frame. I'll have to clean that up and put it pride of place somewhere. What a great find! The window in this room is badly cracked. That will need to be replaced. There's also a fireplace in here. Out of this room and further along the corridor there is a door, which opens out into the kitchen. The kitchen is huge! There are no appliances and there are pipes sticking out and holes all over the walls. It's clearly been brutally stripped at some stage. What is nice though is the old flagstone floor and a big dust-covered red aga in the chimneybreast. Wouldn't it be great to get it working again?!

Terracotta tiles go up the walls. This will be a great room. We could cook here and also have people eat in here as well. A big long wooden dining table with benches on either side would be perfect. This is all going to cost a fortune. There is a backdoor leading to the jungle outside. I'll leave that for another day. Now time to explore upstairs! The staircase is so lovely. Not ornate but curved and smooth. On the wallpaper there are marks were there would have been frames. Maybe photographs. Family photos and portraits, I suppose. Such a shame that they aren't still there. It would have been lovely to see pictures of my ancestors staring out at me. I'd have scanned them for familiar shared features and stories.

At the top of the stairs, there is a long landing which leads to another small staircase. On this floor, there are six bedrooms of ample size and a bathroom. The bathroom is gross. It has a green suite and green tiles on the floor and walls. It's in a cracked, dirty disgusting state. I don't think I'll even walk in there again. I think I'll be washing in the lake for the moment! All the bedrooms have cornicing and ceiling roses and stripped wooden floors. Most have fireplaces. The windows aren't in a good state up here. They are cracked, or completely gone and boarded up. New windows throughout up here! At the end of the corridor and up the little steps there are another two rooms. These are smaller, but still good. Perhaps these were the servants' rooms. This makes it an eight-bedroom house with a bathroom. There's also a hole in the ceiling up here which goes up to the attic. There aren't any stairs or ladders, so I can't take a look, but maybe we can put something up there too.

There's so much to do in the house. It's an absolute mess but it already feels right. Who would have thought that I would ever have an eight-bedroom house! In Dublin this would be worth a lottery win! I shake myself a little. It's hard to believe that this is really happening. This feels like the right place for me, here in the middle of nowhere, beside the water, surrounded by the mountains and energised by the lovely fresh air. I think I can heal here, find myself again and I think I can create something truly wonderful for people to come and enjoy. I am suddenly overwhelmed with contentment. I am lucky to be alive. I've had a lucky escape from a bad relationship, a job that I didn't love and the madness of the city. I'm thankful I took this different path. It started with pain and sadness but now has left me totally free and in this amazing place.

I don't want to lose this feeling of peace. I want to just be with this feeling and enjoy it for longer so I make my way back down the stairs, out the front door, through the jungle of the garden and throw my coat down on the grass between the house and the lake and I sit. I put myself in lotus pose because it just feels like the right thing to do. I put my hands on my knees and take the deepest of breath and then exhale long and nourishingly. With my eyes closed I listen to the lapping of the water, the birds singing sweetly, the breeze rustling the leaves of the trees, I hear a bell somewhere far away, maybe a cowbell. Otherwise it is still. No cars, buses, people, chatter, TV. It's just nature. The quiet sounds of nature babbling along. I open my eyes, heavy as though from sleep and I drink it all in. So beautiful. So calm. I am so blessed. This is my home now, lucky me!

I am interrupted from my peace by a gruff voice shouting, "Bollocks, the flaming hippies have landed. That better not be my new gaffer. I'm not working for some nutty hippy chick." I gather myself up to my five seven height and give my new friend a filthy look.

"My name is Ellie, you must be Leo, my new builder?" Leo, doesn't look the least bit bothered by my dirty look and stares around distractedly.

"You've got a lot of work to do here. The house is in a right state and the outside needs drainage put in and lots of landscaping. It could be nice when it's finished, but it's not going to be cheap. I've done you an itemised list so that you can see the scale of the work."

He hands me a scary looking excel sheet. I glance over it but hone in on the all-important total cost. It's a deep breath moment for sure but actually less than I feared. I have just enough to cover it from my payoff money.

"Okay, Leo, when do we start?" I say with as confident a smile as I can muster. He is a little thrown by this.

"Not to do myself out of cash, but you really should negotiate the price a little, maybe ask for references of my work, ask some questions…" I feel pretty stupid and hot embarrassed redness rises on my cheeks. Leo's eyes wrinkle at the edges and soften, as does his voice, "How about I knock five percent off that total? Also, I'm thinking that you'll need somewhere to stay?"

I nod, looking down like a daft child. "Right, well you can stay in my daughters B&B down the road. It's handy, she could do with the trade and you need a bed. What do you say? Do we have a deal?" I nod.

"Actually hang on, you're not building a hippie commune thing here are you? Because if you are, I can't have any part of that!"

I laugh, "No commune, I promise. It will be a Yoga School. It's just like a normal college but it'll teach yoga."

Leo doesn't seem wholly convinced, but he nods and tells me to follow his van to the B&B. As I drive away from the house, I admire my lot in the rear-view mirror. I'm going to open a Yoga School. Yes, I am! Thank God for Leo with the gruff voice and his dislike of hippies!

Chapter Thirteen
Messages

Ben and I are in constant contact. We message all day and then FaceTime when we can, but the time difference is a pain. He is the one that usually bears the brunt of this by taking calls whenever he can, sometimes in the middle of the night. This morning, I woke up to a number of messages from him as he's been working all day, while I've been asleep.

Ben
02.30 a.m.
Good morning Ellie. You are sleeping soundly I hope. I can imagine your head on the pillow. Big Smile x.

03.32 a.m.
Running a workshop today on Mindfulness. I'll send you my materials. You might be able to use them for the school x.

06.05 a.m.
Amazing food in this place. Afternoon break was tea and cakes. Delish! Thought of you x.

Ellie
07.31am
You've been busy while I've been sleeping! Would love the mindfulness notes…and the cake! Good morning Ben xo

Ben
07.32am
xo

Ellie
07.34am
xoxo

Ben
07.35am
xoxoxo

Ellie
07.38am
xoxoxoxo

Ben
07.51am
xoxoxoxoxoxoxoxoxoxoxoxoxoxoxoxoxoxoxoxoxoxoxox oxoxoxoxoxoinfinity! Now I must do a tiny bit of work or they won't pay me! Haha!

Ellie
07.52am
All work and no play…

Ben
07.53am
Without you, I am a dull boy. When are you coming back?

Ellie
07.54am
Awhhhhhhhhhhhhhhhhh! Sorry I am distracting you. I will stop.

Ben
08.53am

Don't stop. Please. Please. Please. Don't stop.
Ellie
09.30am
xxxxxxxxxxxxxxx

Ben
11.01am
I wish you were here x

Ellie
12.02pm
Me too

Ben
12.30pm
Eleven thirty here. Have another early start tomorrow. Night night, beautiful xoxox.

Ellie
12.50pm
Night lovely man. Sleep well xoxoxo

Chapter Fourteen
Getting Ready

Leo, the builder, came as a recommendation from the local solicitor and it turned out to be a godsend. He and his crew of local lads work their socks off on the house and quickly make progress. I help out onsite a bit, but more often than not, I'm a hindrance rather than a help. I spend more of my time at the B&B planning. The B&B is like home from home. Leo's daughter, Annette, gave me the Cowshed room which as the name suggests, is a converted cowshed. It's really quirky and cosy. It has a tiny kitchen, which suits me just fine for rustling up soup, noodles and the like. Anytime I fancy a substantial feed, I head to the chippie or the local pub, which does great hearty pub grub.

Annette is lovely. She has quickly become a good friend. Her husband Alan is a great cook. He's originally from Dublin, and trained as a chef from the age of sixteen. He does the breakfasts in the B&B and it's seriously the best breakfast I've ever had. After some cajoling, he has agreed to be my chef in the yoga school. He will still do the B&B breakfast, so he'll be busy. Our breakfast will be after the first Yoga session at 8 am, and will be a continental, light affair. He can set that up quickly and go back home to do his work there before coming back to sort lunch and dinner at the school.

Starting a yoga school from scratch is a mountainous task. I really had no idea. I am enjoying the challenge, but it's relentless. I've been to enough retreats, classes and yoga schools to know what I like and how I want to run it, but the reality of organising everything from the curriculum to the teacher recruitment to ordering the loo rolls is tough. It's much tougher than any job I've ever done because all the responsibility is on me. However, it's also the most satisfying thing that I have ever done because it's all mine and I don't have to ask anyone else's opinion. There is no asshole boss to persuade or moronic board to please.

I have managed to convince some amazing teachers to join me on this adventure. Millie, a Kundalini Yoga Specialist and Reiki Master, Isaiah an Ayurveda chef and herbalist. Martha, a Hatha Yoga teacher, with years of experience and Sabel, a holistic therapist, who trained in India in a famous Ashram. I know all of them. I've met them over the years in classes and at various retreats that I have been to myself. This little crew, and I will form the first faculty of the Yoga School. They are due to start arriving in one month's time.

Our first batch of students arrive just two weeks later. Bloody hell! I have so much to do. Our diploma will enable the students to operate as a holistic therapists, yoga teachers, Reiki practitioners or herbalists. It's the only course like it in Europe. The diploma will actually come from the University of Ulster, therefore I have had a lot of communication with them about the curriculum. Because of the amount of content that we cover, it is a residential five-month course and it is a serious level of commitment to extract yourself from your life for five months and move to Donegal. So far I have five students signed up. The dormitories could take a maximum of fifteen students at a time, but I am hoping for ten students for the first course, so that we can find our way. I have budgeted to have ten non-fee-paying students, if I can't get the numbers for the first course, but I have been pleasantly surprised that we've had five unsolicited signups. These came from listings I put on Yoga Retreat websites. I have a whole marketing strategy in my head (given I'm a marketer), but for now I just need to focus on getting the doors open. I need to get up and running quickly before my little pot of cash runs out. I know the first few courses will not be perfect, I will have lots of learning as I go to do but that's life. I am a perfectionist by nature, so anything less than perfect on anything has historically been hard for me to accept of myself or anyone else. However, I had a great boss once who told me that my seventy percent was someone else's hundred percent and that I needed to learn to get things go at that seventy percent. I thought he was crazy at first but slowly I tried the logic and realised that he was right. People still thought my seventy percent output was brilliant, therefore I learnt to push and punish myself less and in doing so, have more time for other things. That time led me to yoga and yoga led me in a roundabout, obstacle course way to here. I probably owe that old boss a drink or at thc very least a big thank-you.

I'm currently sitting on my bed with paperwork everywhere, and my laptop in front of me. There is a gentle knock at my door. I leave the door open in the day. It's that kind of place. It's Annette. I see her abundance of blonde curls before her. Her curls are proper corkscrew ones that can only make you smile and will, I suspect, keep her forever young. She has a rosy, wide smile and sparkly green eyes to match her lovely warm personality. She has a little floral tray in hand and there is a waft of something delicious.

"Food for the worker!" Alan has been baking for Penny's playdate later. Penny is their energetic, adorable, little, five-year-old. "I thought you might fancy some homemade chocolate cookies."

I'm delighted, "Oh wow! Would I ever! Give them here! Honestly, if Alan wasn't already happily married, I would snap him up."

I tuck happily into them, "These are amazing. I'll have to get him to do them for the yoga school on winter evenings. We could serve them with hot chocolate."

Annette laughs, "Hot chocolate and cookies sounds like my kind of class! Sign me up!"

We both laugh easily. Annette has this effect on everyone. She is so relaxed. Her vibe is infectious. "Do you fancy a drink in the pub tonight? Mum and Dad are looking after the kids, so we are making a bid for freedom."

"Are you sure that you don't want some time to yourselves? You don't want Ellie, the third wheel with you surely?"

Annette raises an eyebrow, "Do you really think we're out for a romantic night in McCormacks' pub? I'd kill Alan if that was his idea of a date! He'll be chatting to his friends most of the time, come on. It'll be good to get out. You've been working too hard. Your light is on before we're up and long after we go to bed. You need a night off."

She's right. I have been working like a woman possessed, but there is a never-ending list of stuff to do. Every time I think I'm getting somewhere; I remember ten other things that I had forgotten about. A few hours away from it all, a drink and a gossip might be just what I need.

McCormacks' is busy. It always is, being the only watering hole in the village. Pete and Amy the owners are a lovely jovial couple. They are perfect publicans, warm and welcoming to all. I opt for a hot whisky, as I feel a cold brewing and want to nip it in the bud. My builder lads are at the corner of the bar, so I send a round their way which is met with a roar of approval and enthusiastic waves and thumbs up. Even Leo touches his cap to me. A good move to keep the workers happy. Pete the barman gently smacks his head, "Ellie, I'm so sorry, there was a guy in earlier, looking for you. He said he was a good friend of yours. He was waffling on for ages about you, so I presumed he was friend and sent him in the direction of the yoga school or the B&B. Amy was livid when I told her, as she said I could have been sending an axe murder or some weirdo right to you. Did he find you?"

I'm surprised that anyone would be looking for me. "No, he didn't but don't worry, I'm sure he wasn't an axe murderer. Did he give his name?"

Pete shakes his head, "Sorry no and I didn't think to ask. Amy would have. He was a good-looking fella, dark hair and eyes. Does that ring any bells?"

It did. Could it be? No! Ben? Could Ben have come to see me as a surprise? My insides are leaping and fluttering like crazy. We've been emailing, Whatsapping and FaceTiming each other constantly since Australia, but he's never mentioned coming to visit imminently. I am so excited that he might be here. Please let him me here! I quickly fill Annette in and say my goodbyes. I have to get back to the B&B. The thought of him there or nearby renders me incapable of having a sensible conversation.

It's a short walk back to the B&B. I see the smoke from the fireplace curling above the swaying oak trees before I see the house. It's a gorgeous old farmhouse. The guys have put a lot of love and care into it. There is a car at the front that wasn't there when we left. I can't make out the type or color in the dark, but it definitely wasn't there before. The car is empty so the owner must be inside. Ben is inside! Oh wow! I feel like I might burst with excitement and nerves. I tuck my hair behind my ears and take a deep breath before pushing the front door open. I can hear voices in the kitchen, so I make my way there.

"Oh my God!" I stammer, feeling suddenly faint and like all the blood and energy has dropped to my feet. It's not Ben. It's Alex.

Chapter Fifteen
Crossed Wires

Alex rushes forward, kisses my cheek and hugs me before I can swat him away. "Oh, Ellie, it's so good to see you. You look incredible."

I gather myself and shrug him off, going to the kettle to make a tea to busy my shaking hands.

"What are you doing here? How did you even know where I was?"

"I've been looking for you Ellie, asking your friends where you are, going to your favourite haunts. No one had seen you. I was so worried. So, I went down to your Mum and Dad's thinking that you might be there. Your mum told me where I could find you."

I silently curse my parents, especially my mother who probably silenced Dad. How could she (a) send him here and (b) not warn me? I could kill her!

I am enraged, panicked and something else…I am so, so, disappointed that it wasn't Ben.

"I still don't understand why you're here Alex. I don't want to see you…clearly!" Pete's Mum, who has been tidying up the kitchen, suddenly realises that this is not a happy reunion. She looks at me with shrewd eyes, "Ellie, are you okay? Shall I call the pub and get Pete to come?"

I smile tiredly at her so that she knows it's okay, "It's okay, Jean, he won't be staying long." Jean gives Alex a filthy look and retreats to the living-room which is still within earshot.

"I will just be in the next room if you need me sweetheart."

Alex looks annoyed, "Who's this Pete?" This fares my temper, "Seriously, you're having a go at me about a man. You have no right. None at all. You forfeited any right when you shagged half the office on our kitchen island unit!"

I'm screaming now. Totally incensed. Jean must be beside herself in the next room. Who needs EastEnders when you've got me staying! Alex is still angry looking, "It wasn't half the office. You never let me explain. You just ran away like you always do. I have been devastated, Ellie. I made a mistake, a big one, but I miss you. I love you. Please let me explain. Please give us a chance again."

He must be nuts. How can he possibly think that I would want him back? Suddenly Pete bursts into the house out of breath. His mum must have phoned him and he's run back. Bless him. Annette follows running soon after. Pete is a big lad and kind of out of shape, so he bends hands on his knees panting. Between pants he manages, "You must be, Alex. Get out of my house."

Alex glows red and balls his fists in anger. He lunges at Pete and knocks him against the kitchen units then starts punching him in face. "We've just broken up. You stay away from her. She's still mine." Annette and Jean look stricken, clearly thinking that he's accusing Pete of being with me and wondering if it's true. Oh God. Oh God. Please. Pete might be out of shape but he's not taking this lying down. He gets up and lamps Alex's back, hard. There is another noise at the door and Leo walks in. Quickly appraising the situation, he grabs Alex by the neck in a lock and lifts him clean off the ground and carries him outside. We hear him throw him to the ground, some whispered mumbling, and then the front door bang closed. Leo reappears and pats Pete down. Checking him over. "You all right lad?"

Pete looks sheepish, like he wishes his father-in-law didn't just walk in on him fighting. Pete nods. Leo then turns his attention to me. "I presume that was the young fella who messed you about in Dublin?"

I have never mentioned it to Leo. We don't have that kind of relationship. Perhaps Annette told him. Leo continues, "I told him that if he ever comes near you again that I'll chop his balls off and leave him to bleed to death in the bog, where no one will hear his cries for help. He got into his flashy car sharpish, so I don't think he'll be back." My Dad would never say something like that but in this moment I'm so grateful. "Thanks, Leo. And Annette, there's nothing going on with me and Pete. Alex was just looking for trouble and misunderstood the situation. I hope we're okay."

Annette has been cuddling up to Pete while Leo was talking, so I presume it's all okay. "Ah, Ellie, sure I know. Pete would never. You would never. Jean, can you pop the kettle on. I think we all need a cuppa."

Jean is quiet as we drink our tea, and I can tell she's shell shocked. She pulls me aside, "Ellie, I knew that you had a back breakup, but I didn't know the details of it. You are a beautiful, smart, kind young girl with your whole life ahead of you. Do not go back to that man darling. He is bad news. Don't be with anyone who doesn't treat you like a queen. Look at Pete and Annette. Leo and I. Leo might be a bit brusque, but do you know that before he leaves for work each day he makes me breakfast and leaves it on a tray by my bed and kisses me on the cheek before tiptoeing out, so as not to wake me. I know he adores me. Never be with anyone who doesn't make you feel like a queen to your core. Will you promise me Ellie?"

She is serious in her advice and I take it, accepting it as it was given—seriously.

I am thoroughly exhausted when I go back to the cowshed. I throw my clothes on the floor, not bothering to tidy up and get straight into my most comfortable PJs. I make myself a hot chocolate for comfort and get into bed. My work and laptop are scattered all over the bed. I just push them aside. Retrieving my phone from my bag I check my WhatsApp messages looking for Ben. I've not checked it since before going to the pub. I see there are lots of messages in there from him and he is really cross. "How could you not tell me that you are back with Alex? How could you string me along like this? I thought we were serious about each other. I have been making plans to change my life to be with you. How could you do this?"

I'm so confused. How could he think that I was back with Alex? It's an odd coincidence that Alex was here and now Ben is so upset. I rack my brain then quickly grab my laptop open and check my FaceTime. There! A call from Ben at eight pm which was answered. The call lasted for two minutes. I didn't take that call. Could Alex have been in my room and accepted the call? It seems unlikely, but not beyond the realms of possibility. I immediately try to FaceTime Ben. No answer. I call his mobile. No answer. His house phone. No answer. Fuck! He must be ignoring me. I'll have to message him. "Ben, I don't know what happened that made you think that Alex and I are together. We are not. *Definitely* not. He showed up here tonight unexpectedly and I sent him away. I didn't want to see him. I don't want to see him ever again. Please talk to me. Please let me know you are okay?"

After I've sent it I stare at my phone and keep refreshing Whatsapp. Eventually the tick turns blue and I can see he's read it and is online. I wait and wait. He's typing. Now stopped. He's typing again. Now stopped. I keep checking for a response, but after forty minutes I'm feeling deflated and oh so tired. I lie down, thoughts reeling in my head. Why is my life so complicated? Why can't things go smoothly for once? I really thought I was making progress with the Yoga school and with Ben, but maybe I'm just kidding myself. I fall asleep because I am utterly wiped out. I am woken by the flashing of my laptop and a ringing. It's FaceTime. It's Ben. I click and accept the call still lying down. "Hello" my voice is groggy and sleepy.

"I woke you. I'm sorry love. I went to see a friend to drown my sorrows and then saw your message and rushed home to call you. To see you."

His sweetness, his voice, his face makes me sob. I miss him. I wish he was here. "Oh, Ellie please don't cry. It was a misunderstanding. It's okay now."

I shake my head, "It's not though is it? You live on the other side of the world. I live in the back end of nowhere and am opening a business. How can this work? I've fallen in love with someone I can't have. I can't be hurt again. Not after last time. I just can't take it. It will break me."

I'm really sobbing now.

"You love me?"

I nod over and over looking at him. He nods back mimicking my movement, which makes me laugh. "That's better. There's my girl. Wow. You're so beautiful. How lucky am I? Ellie, I love you too. So very much. I have been thinking about you constantly from the very first moment I saw you."

I start sobbing again. This time it's a happy sob mixed with little smiles. "Ellie, I know this seems so hard and impossible right now, but we can't find each other and then just forgot we have and let it go. Trust that things will work out. Can you do that?"

I wipe my eyes and sigh deeply, "The universe hasn't been good to me in the past, Ben. It really hasn't. I don't have any trust left that things will work out in the end because they should."

Ben is quiet for a moment, thinking. "Okay, don't trust in the universe. Trust in me. Ellie, can you do that? Trust me that I will make this work out in the end?"

He looks so beautiful, so intense.

He really means it, so I nod. But, in my heart I am not convinced.

It transpires that Alex did, in fact, answer the call on my laptop. Ben asked who he was and where I was. Alex said his name and that he was my boyfriend come to visit me at my new venture. He asked if he could take a message. The nerve of him to be in my room, to answer my laptop and to assume he could just pick up where he left off. Unbelievable for most people, but Alex is used to getting whatever he wants therefore unsurprising for him really.

I'm not sure what will happen between Ben and I. I'm besotted and I don't doubt his feelings, but the odds seem stacked against us in terms of the geography. I love Australia to visit, but my soul is here in Ireland. This is my home, and this Yoga school means everything to me. This is where I need to be. Ben has a career and a whole life in Australia and can't just up sticks and move here in the hope that it will work out with a girl he barely knows. So my hopes are low for our future, but I am relieved that we sorted out the mix up and that we finally admitted our feelings. I love him and he loves me.

Chapter Sixteen
Class of 2018

As my first class sit before me on the very first day of the yoga school, I gaze at their enthusiastic, open faces and feel excited and proud. I am full of contentment and determination to make this a success. They seem like an interesting bunch of people. I can't wait to get to know them and help them on their journey.

Melanie, 27, is a beautician and fitness fanatic. She wants to add to her skills and eventually open her own holistic salon. She is single and lives with her Teddy Dog, Leo, in Cork. Sara, 37, is a primary school teacher and is taking a sabbatical from work. She wants to bring yoga and holistic therapies into her school and other schools in the area. She lives in Galway with her husband Ian.

Mark, 19, has just finished college and is taking a year out before university. His family is very alternative. He has grown up practicing yoga and traveling around the world with his parents. An only child, he is going to miss his Mum, but he wants to retreat from the world for a while, before starting his formal studies again.

Alex, 62, is an architect from Dublin. He has three grown children and was recently widowed a year ago. Like Mark, he wants to retreat from the world. He doesn't want a change of career but he needs time out for himself. His late wife Liz was from Donegal, so he feels that coming here to the Yoga school will help him find himself again and connect with her.

Beth, 17, is a force of nature from Waterford. She has wanted to be a yoga teacher for as long as she can remember. She takes yoga extremely seriously and is itching to begin her teaching career. I can already see that she will be a brilliant teacher, which is incredible for someone so young. Ingrid, 56, is a gorgeous French lady from Nice, who has been living in London for years with her son. She is beautiful inside and out. Her reasons for being here are not clear to me yet as she seems quite shy and reluctant to divulge too much about herself, but I feel that she will be a wonderful addition to the group.

Clodagh, 28, an actress from Dublin. She is quite well known as she had a role in a well-known drama. Her character was killed off the show six months ago, and she is finding it had to get work. Additional to this, she has recently finished with her long-term boyfriend who is another well-known Irish actor. She ended things after he was photographed with a woman in a compromising situation. She is feeling vulnerable and bruised so wants to take time off and focus on doing something for herself. Given my recent situation, I understand how she is feeling and really hope we can help her.

Steve, 37, is an IT manager from London. He says that he is a geek. I think he's a funny, quirky guy with a broad range of interests. He is incredibly talented and excels in his work. He likes to take contracts and work hard for six months, and then take time off to do something fun or relaxing. Yoga, Reiki and Herbalism are on his to do list, therefore our course is perfect for him.

Lexi, 32, is a stuntwoman from the US. Amazing job. Cool as hell lady. She wants to add yoga to her skill set. Her grandparents were from Donegal, so in addition to the course, she is also going to look for her relatives and work on her family tree while she is here. Thomas, 35, from Australia is also booked on the course, but he has not arrived yet, so I don't know his story.

I wanted ten students for the first course and here we are. It feels so good to be here. I have written three different welcome speeches. I want to get it right. As I stand here, I abandon the last draft and decide to speak from the heart instead. “Welcome to the Yoga School. We are so glad to have you here. I, and the teachers have prepared an incredible, jam-packed curriculum for you. This course is the first of its kind in Europe. We aim to send you off with the skills and confidence to have successful careers in holistic therapy, as well as, becoming more healthy, physically and emotionally. I thank you from the bottom of my heart for choosing to study with us. We will repay that trust with boundless energy and passion for you. Enjoy, work hard and love life. Namaste.”

The room is filled with clapping and smiling. I am on a high. The moment is interrupted by the doorbell ringing. I installed one with a Tibetan chime, so that it didn’t disrupt the vibe of the school. Annette who has been watching at the door, signals that she will get it. The room is a babble of excited chatter. Annette comes back and smiles broadly at me. She gestures for me to come over. “Your final student has arrived. I think you’ll be happy.”

I laugh, “No matter how hot he is, I couldn’t date a student.”

Annette shrugs, still smiling. I move into the hall and see a guy with his back to me. On hearing my footsteps he turns. Oh my heart! It’s Ben! He is smiling even more broadly than Annette and judging by the amount of luggage he has with him, I think he’ll be staying. I run and jump into a hug, legs around his waist. He spins me around and nuzzles into my neck.

“Thomas?” I say. He laughs his gorgeous laugh, “It’s my second name. My full name is Benjamin Thomas Aiken.”

I’m so happy I think I could fly, “So Benjamin Thomas Aiken, how long are you here for?”

He gently puts me on the ground and cups my face like he did the last time he saw me. Ever so softly he says, “Forever, if you’ll have me?”